OTTO A
HIMML

'Our love ... the ages. We ... manic Romeo a...

Reichsführer SS Heinrich Himmler to his mistress 'Gertrud', 1 Jan, 1945. (From H. Trevor-Roper (Ed): *The Himmler Letters*, Oxford University Press, 1983.)

Also by Leo Kessler

The *SS Assault Regiment Wotan* Series
SS PANZER BATTALION
DEATH'S HEAD
CLAWS OF STEEL
GUNS AT CASSINO
THE DEVIL'S SHIELD
HAMMER OF THE GODS
FORCED MARCH
BLOOD AND ICE
THE SAND PANTHERS
COUNTER-ATTACK
PANZER HUNT
SLAUGHTER GROUND
HELLFIRE
FLASHPOINT
CAULDRON OF BLOOD
SCHIRMER'S HEADHUNTERS
WHORES OF WAR
SCHIRMER'S DEATH LEGION

The *Stormtroop* Series
STORMTROOP
BLOOD MOUNTAIN
VALLEY OF THE ASSASSINS
RED ASSAULT
HIMMLER'S GOLD
FIRE OVER KABUL
WAVE OF TERROR
EAGLES IN THE SNOW
FIRE OVER AFRICA

The *Otto Stahl* Series
OTTO'S PHONEY WAR
OTTO'S BLITZKRIEG!
OTTO AND THE REDS
OTTO AND THE YANKS
OTTO AND THE SS

Leo Kessler

Otto Stahl 6
Otto and the Himmler Love Letters

Futura

A Futura BOOK

First published in Great Britain in 1984
by Futura Publications, a Division of
Macdonald & Co (Publishers) Ltd
London & Sydney

ISBN 0 7088 2561 3

Typeset, printed and bound in Great Britain by
Hazell Watson & Viney Limited,
Member of the BPCC Group
Aylesbury, Bucks

Futura Publications
A Division of
Macdonald & Co (Publishers) Ltd
Maxwell House
74 Worship Street
London EC2A 2EN
A BPCC plc Company

Author's Introduction

I suppose there is no one in the Western hemisphere today who does not know about last year's sensational discovery of the 'Himmler Love Letters'? Even though the *Stern's* so-called 'Hitler Diaries' had proved to be a cunning fake only months earlier, 'The Letters', as they soon became called, were accepted at once and became an instant success.

As everyone knows as soon as the Sunday newspaper, the *News of the World*, announced it possessed 'The Letters' and Mr David Irving, the celebrated German scholar, testified they were absolutely genuine[1], BBC TV instantly secured world film rights, narrowly beating Mr Francis Coppola of *Godfather* fame in the bidding. Their subsequent semi-historical documentary – *Heinrich and Gertrud: a Nazi Love Affair* – with Lord Olivier and Miss Barbara Windsor in the title roles was a tremendous success.

Even beyond the Iron Curtain, 'The Letters' created a sensation. *Novy Mir* printed them in full, in a pirated edition, of course; though it must be recorded that this celebrated Moscow journal *did* offer Miss Windsor a free holiday on the Black Sea as a strange form of recompense[2]. Indeed *Pravda* itself quoted several of Himmler's letters (beneath the annual report on the output of tractors in Outer Mongolia, it must be admitted) and used them to launch a bitter attack on the 'decadence and corruption of Western Society, past *and* present'. The reference to Miss Windsor's celebrated topless appearance on the beach at

[1] See *D. Irving: How the Letters were Discovered by Me*, Futura Books, 1983. pp 42. Price £2.50.

[2] See the *Sun* (Monday 2 Nov, 1983). *Barbara Bares All on Black Sea! Exclusive Pix!*

Yalta is all too obvious. Unfortunately, that staid Party paper did not publish any photographs of those well-known 'mammaliarian objects', as *Pravda* put it delicately, which it alleged so shocked a delegation of Moscow bus-drivers, who were attending the Fraternal World Congress in Yalta, that they 'spontaneously and unanimously' refused to meet the British delegation from the Greater London Area, led by Mr Kenneth Livingstone.

Yes, there are few, in both East and West, who have not chuckled at 'Harrykins' ' note to his 'Little Mother' of 3 December, 1943, urging her to wear (her) 'thickest woolly things next to your pretty private parts'. Apparently the *Reichsführer* SS even sent his mistress, 'My Little Mother' as he was wont to address her on paper, supplementary clothing coupons in case she did not possess the requisite woollen knickers. In all things, Heinrich 'Harrykins' Himmler was *sehr korrekt*.

So far, however, there has only been Mr David Irving's account of how he acted as an intermediary for the *News of the World* in the purchase of the letters from 'an unknown elderly German in a trenchcoat and black hat, who might well have worked for the legendary Otto Skorzeny'[1].

But who was that 'elderly German in a trenchcoat and black hat who might well have once worked for the legendary Otto Skorzeny', the man who provided the *News of the World* with its biggest scoop ever, since that Sunday when it revealed that one of Queen Victoria's sons was Jack the Ripper?

I think I know who handed Mr Irving those letters written on poor, yellowing, wartime paper under the clock at St Pancras Station, as agreed upon that rainy Monday morning in the autumn of last year. Didn't Mr Irving describe the unknown's eyes as being 'bright-blue and intelligent with the look of a man who had never missed a trick in the whole of his long and undoubtedly somewhat crooked life'? Those eyes are, for me, a clear indication of who Mr Irving had been dealing with that morning. His description, too, of his con-

[1] See: 'Skorzeny Man Probable Source of Himmler Letters', *The Sunday Times, Insight*, 15 October, 1983.

versation with the unknown was a further clue to the German's identity. 'With a crooked, disarming smile'[1], he had reeled off his conditions to the *News of the World*'s representative, 'like a fast-talking life assurance salesman', promising that the letters would be sensational, full of 'sex and sadism', throwing a completely new light on the private life of the 'most feared man in Europe'. Who else could sound like a cheap publisher's publicity blurb for his last 'block-buster' than – *Herr Otto Stahl*!

Yes, dear reader, Otto Stahl, whose wartime experiences I have been detailing over these last three or four years as his only authorized biographer. Although Herr Stahl disappeared from his Spanish seaside home – my exile, as he was wont to call it somewhat melodramatically – so suddenly, as soon as the *News of the World* had paid over that enormous sum of money for 'The Letters', I now have enough evidence in my possession to reveal the true story behind the sensational events of last year. A few pieces of the jigsaw still elude me (naturally Herr Stahl was playing the whole business with his cards close to his chest), but this is, in essence, the true account of how Otto, the Count and Marty MacTavish, the future owner of the 'Jewish Mills & Boon' publishing company (as he liked to describe his New York firm), tracked Himmler down in the last months of World War Two[2].

It is, I fear, not a pretty tale, but in that terrible spring of 1945, when Hitler's vaunted 'One Thousand Year Reich' fell apart, there were not many pretty things happening. Here, then, is the true story of how Otto Stahl and his comrades came to possess those celebrated Himmler Letters . . .

L.K.

[1] Mr Irving in a BBC *Panorama* interview, Monday 16 October. Quoted in A. Benn's *They March Again*! Century Publishing Co. 1984.

[2] An enlightening and highly interesting account of Mr M. MacTavish's post-war career as a New York publisher is to be found in the *Washington Post* article (22 November, 1983) entitled: 'Schmaltz, Shekels and Schiksas – Long Live the Yiddische Momma!'

BOOK ONE: THE CHASE IS ON

'C'est magnifique, mais ce n'est pas la guerre.'

Marshall Bosquet

ONE

The killers came just before curfew.

They appeared no different from the other grey, beaten civilians who were now barring their doors and closing their shutters for the long March night. They were shabby, undernourished, dressed in cast-off clothes, hugging the lengthening shadows like grey rats. There were only two things that marked them off from the rest of the people in this defeated town with its war-shattered buildings and the white flags of surrender hanging everywhere – the look of fanatical hate in their downcast eyes and the automatic pistols that they gripped in the pockets of their shabby grey coats.

Now the Rhenish town was almost silent. Up front there was the pink flickering of the permanent barrage and the soft, muted rumble of the guns. Somewhere a jeep was groaning in low gear through the deserted streets. It would be an American patrol. Any German caught on the streets now that curfew had been sounded would be automatically arrested. A week ago when the Amis had first arrived, they had shot anyone found outside after dark. The bearded, begrimed frontline troops had been a rough, tough bunch. They had looted, raped and shot, terrorizing the little town for forty-eight hours before they had moved on again, pushing ever closer to the Rhine. Now the town had settled down once more. It had a military government office and a German mayor once again. The only troops in the place now were men from the US supply service and a handful of MPs[1]. Still, the killers were taking no chances. They had not come so far and suffered so many hardships in order to be thwarted at the very last moment before they had carried out their mission. It was vital that they should succeed this night.

[1] Military Police.

'Snowdrops – quick!' their leader, a gaunt giant of a youth, who could not have been older than sixteen, hissed. '*Los*!'

As one, trained killers all, they vaulted over a wall and dropped onto the floor of the ruined house beyond. Even the girl cleared it easily. A moment later the jeep crawled round the corner, a white-helmeted American military policeman moving the spotlight from side to side like a single, restless, baleful eye.

The youthful killers froze. Their hands gripping the pistols were suddenly wet with sweat. They hardly dared breathe. The gaunt youth, who was their leader, felt for his grenade. If they were discovered, he would throw it straight at the jeep. His fingers found the cotter-pin and held it tight. The jeep was almost parallel with their hiding place. They waited, hearts thumping away painfully. *Would they be discovered?*

The hard white light flashed over them. It seemed to linger a long while and they felt naked and terribly exposed. In a moment there would be the excited shout, the alarm, the challenge and then it would begin. Nothing happened. The light moved on and the jeep continued to groan its way down the street. Nevertheless they did not move immediately. There could be a foot patrol following the jeep. Deliberately, the gaunt youth made himself count up to sixty before slowly raising his head above the wall. The street was empty. There was no foot patrol and the jeep had gone. The youth stifled his sigh of relief. The others, even the girl, would mock any weakness he might show. Instead, he grunted as casual as could be, '*Los*, let's get on with it. They've gone!'

Like grey ghosts they continued their silent progress down the empty streets, their feet making no sound in the thick white dust from the bombing which covered them. Once they had marched proudly down these same streets, singing lustily, their flags fluttering bravely in the breeze, the cheers of the admiring crowds echoing and re-echoing in the stone chasms. And those same civilians who had once cheered them had now become scared, fawning little people, who jumped fearfully every time the Amis gave an order. So the killers had come back, sneaking into their own city, to murder one of their own race, their own blood.

'Adolf Hitler Platz,' the girl said to the gaunt youth.

'No longer, comrade,' he answered sourly, pausing momentarily to get his bearings. He laughed softly. It was not a pleasant sound. 'Now the traitors call it General Eisenhower Platz. Those lick-spittles learn fast.' He spat into the dust and moved on. 'Our Führer, Adolf Hitler, deserves a better people.'

'They will learn, comrade, they will learn what happens to traitors,' the girl said fervently.

The gaunt youth nodded, but said no more, concentrating on the task at hand. They were getting closer to the street in which the traitor lived. Now nothing must go wrong.

The Venloerstrasse had survived the last terrible years of bombing better than most. Some of the big nineteenth century villas, set back in their park-like gardens, had lost their roofs or were patched up with tar paper and wooden boards, but they were all occupied. The gaunt youth could tell that from the notices stuck up on every gate listing the names of each occupant, as those swine of the Ami military administration demanded: and here and there he could catch a snatch of muted conversation or the sound of a radio, probably all tuned to London or Luxembourg these days. What a pack they were, these civilians! They made no attempt to keep contact, even by radio, with their brothers on the other side of the line, who still fought on bravely for the holy cause of the Fatherland and final victory.

'It must be around here,' the girl broke into his bitter thoughts. 'If I remember correctly, the fat swine lived about here.'

The gaunt youth stopped. He pulled out his little pencil flashlight and shone the blue beam on the gate. He flicked it off again. 'Yes, it's his house,' he announced. 'Bodo,' he commanded urgently, his nerves tingling electrically with excitement now, 'into the garden. Karl . . . Dieter, with me . . . You, Karin, you keep watch.'

'But can't I be in . . .'

'No,' he hissed sharply. 'Do your duty. Now move it, the lot of you!'

Hurriedly they took up their positions, automatically fitting the long ugly silencers to their pistols, schoolkids playing cops and robbers, with one difference – these pistols really killed!

Followed by Karl and Dieter, both small, skinny and looking about fourteen, the gaunt youth started to walk up the drive towards the door of the nineteenth century villa, all their gazes fixed on the shutters, ready for the first sign of danger. The three of them could hear the muffled music coming from within. It was hectic, nervous, un-German. 'Ami nigger music,' the one called Karl sneered, face contorted bitterly. 'Not only does the traitor lick their boots, he also listens to their decadent music. *Typisch*!'

The gaunt youth said nothing. He concentrated all his energy on what was soon to come. He'd need all his reserves then. He stopped suddenly. '*Telefon*!' he hissed urgently. 'There.' He pointed in the glowing darkness. 'The Amis gave him a telephone after all.'

'He's their running dog. They give juicy scraps to the dogs which obey them,' Bodo sneered. Without waiting for a command, he took out his knife and sliced through the wire. Even if they were discovered now, the traitor wouldn't be able to summon the Americans to help him – in time.

At the door, the gaunt youth hesitated a moment, then he drew a deep breath and rang the bell. It was starting.

For a moment nothing happened, as the echo of the bell died away in the corridor. Feet began to move towards them, seemingly hesitant, as if reflecting the sudden tension within the house. The gaunt youth, waiting there on the step, could physically feel the occupants' fear, as if all activity within had abruptly ceased and they were asking themselves who was ringing the bell now after curfew. Was it drunken Ami soldiers looking for women again? Or, even worse, their blacks? Or was it something else?

The footsteps ceased. A frightened voice quavered in poor English, 'Who there?'

The gaunt youth made his voice sound humble, beaten, a little afraid, although he was quivering with tension and rage. 'German refugees, *Herr Buergermeister*. A handful of young people from the Eifel, sir . . . Trying to make our way to the Reich and our parents.' He swallowed back his anger. 'We are hungry, sir . . .'

A long silence followed. The killers waited. They could almost feel the traitor's fear, as he stood there behind the closed door, feverishly considering what he should do.

Suddenly Karin's girlish voice broke the heavy brooding night silence. 'I am *so* hungry, sir . . . I haven't eaten since yesterday . . . Please spare us some bread.'

That did it. The girl's voice banished the traitor's fears. They heard the rattle of a chain being undone. A bolt was withdrawn. The gaunt youth tensed. At his side, the other two went into a half crouch as they had been taught. The youth felt his hand gripping the pistol butt, flushed with hot sweat. He tried to calm himself, but failed. His heart was beating like a trip-hammer. He swallowed hard. It was going to happen in exactly one minute.

The door creaked open and a knife of yellow light sliced into the darkness. A fat man in a waistcoat, his feet in battered slippers, stood there, a cigar held in his right hand, blinking at the sudden darkness, trying to take in the faces of the youths before him. Beyond, further down the corridor, the gaunt youth could see a motherly-looking woman with grey hair, hands twisting her apron nervously, as she waited.

For a long moment they all stood thus, like actors frozen in place at the end of some cheap melodrama. The youth seemed unable to move. Then he smelled the aroma of the cigar the fat man held in his hand and rage swept through him. The swine was smoking an Ami cigar! '*Sie sind Herr Buergermeister Klose*?' he demanded, his voice harsh and threatening.

The fat traitor moved back a pace, obviously alarmed by the tone of the question and the sudden hard, burning look in the youth's icy blue eyes. 'Yes . . . yes, of course, I am the burgomaster . . . What . . .' The words died on his lips, as he saw the object the youth held in his hand. 'What . . . what . . .' he stuttered, fat face suddenly quavering with fear.

'What is it, Karl?' his wife called from down the corridor. 'Is there anything wrong, dear?'

'Karl Klose,' the gaunt youth rasped. 'You have been sentenced to death by the High Court of the German Reich. *Reichsführer* Heinrich Himmler has personally signed the death warrant. It is now my duty to carry . . .'

'But what is this?' the traitor stuttered, falling back, face ashen with fear.

'*Karl*!' his wife called. 'Come away from that door. Quick . . .'

'To carry out that sentence,' the youth continued harshly, jaw muscles tightening as he brought up the pistol, aiming it at the traitor's fat stomach, already taking first pressure. 'I now declare this sentence –'

'*NO!*' Klose screamed, throwing up his hands to protect his face. '*PLEASE, NO!*'

The gaunt youth pressed the trigger. A soft plop. Suddenly a steaming hole appeared in the front of the traitor's waistcoat. It started to flush red. The youth fired again – and again. Klose slammed against the wall, false teeth bulging obscenely from abruptly slack-lipped mouth. Slowly, very slowly, as the woman shrieked hysterically, he started to slip down the wall, dead, trailing a smear of red behind him. The three of them waited calmly until he slumped to the floor, then all three fired once more. The traitor's face disappeared and dripped down on his fat chest like red molten wax. Behind them at the gate, the girl jumped up and down with joy, clapping her hands like the excited schoolkid that she really was. Abruptly she remembered her duty. She hastily pulled out her knife and, with her tongue between her lips, started to carve that dread sign of warning on the gate.

A moment later, as the first hurried flares started to hiss into the night sky, setting the dogs off barking hoarsely, they were off into the darkness, running for their lives . . .

TWO

'Has it ever struck you, Count,' Otto Stahl grunted, as he piled up the American ration boxes intended for the front, 'that Germany has produced a nation of nymphos and we German men have never realized it till the kind Amis came along and enlightened us in their usual generous manner.' He spat into the dust of the barracks square.

Count von der Weide, Otto Stahl's comrade ever since 1939[1], straightened up and swept his long grey hair back from his fleshy handsome face, with one of those flamboyant, theatrical gestures to which he was partial. 'I don't quite understand, my dear boy,' he said, frowning at the women who were hanging around the entrance to the American barracks.

Otto gave him that cocky Berlin working-class grin of his. 'Of course you don't, you silly old fart. But I'll tell you this, Count. If things go on here like they are at the moment, virginity is gonna be a collector's item in Germany soon.'

The Count stared at Otto's determined young face, with its keen, intelligent, knowing eyes, and said, 'Do you really think so, Otto?'

Otto wiped the sweat off his brow and neatly palmed another pack of US cigarettes, which brought a small fortune on the black market these days and which were the main reason they were working at this American supply depot. 'I *know* so, Count. Look at that gash.' He indicated the women in their too short floral dresses and high-heeled wooden shoes cluttering up the entrance to the depot, looking longingly at the bored GIs of the 'Red Ball Express'[2]. 'One word and they'd have the pants off every

[1] See *Otto's Phoney War* for further details.

[2] US Army supply organization, taking up supplies to the front.

man-jack of them – for free. See that big one with all the wood in front of the door.'

'I wish you would not use such common working-class expressions, Otto,' the Count reproved his young friend gently. But Otto wasn't listening.

'That one, the Amis call the "garrison cycle" 'cos everyone has ridden her, get it?' He nudged the Count knowingly. 'And she shows her beaver to anybody who wants to have a look at it.'

'Her – *beaver*?' the Count stuttered in bewilderment.

'Her pudding, Count. Don't you know nothing? And she shows it without even asking for a shitting lung-torpedo for the look. Hell, Count, women like that could ruin the whole shitting black market. And, don't forget to put every second pack of Camels in yer pocket.'

'I won't, Otto,' the Count said dutifully and bent with a weary sigh to lift another case of C rations. At the gate one of the camp followers had raised her short skirt, fluttering her artificial eyelashes at the bored GIs provocatively. She wasn't wearing knickers. Otto shook his head. Business was going absolutely to pot. Soon they'd all be like the 'garrison cycle', giving it away . . .

Otto Stahl had decided to take 'a dive' as he called it, the day the Americans first reached the Rhine near Dusseldorf three weeks earlier. '*Der Traum ist aus*,' he had announced to the girls, as they collected around him in the main room of the '1st Mobile Brothel (Other Ranks Only)', with the guns thundering across the valley. 'The dream's over. The clock's well and truly in the pisspot! The Amis will have reached the whole length of the Rhine by the end of this week, and then, girls, your services will no longer be needed.'

There were cries of alarm and protest from the assembled girls, or 'co-workers', as Otto preferred to call them.

He held up his hands for silence. 'No, co-workers, I must insist. I will not allow your bodies to be soiled by the perverted paws of the Anglo-American gangsters. What honest man would tolerate a brave German girl, who has given her all for the Fatherland, being groped by the hands of those decadent enemy swine? *Never*!'

He looked fiercely at them, while the Count, old fool that he was, nodded his stern approval. 'Hear, hear,' he declared fervently.

'Knock it off, you perverted banana-sucker,' Titty-Roll Roberta cried, those massive breasts of hers, for which she was justly famous throughout the Greater German Wehrmacht, shaking like jellies with indignation. 'How are we gonna keep body and soul alive without work? That's all we know – the old mattress polka and the two-backed beast.'

'Too true, Titty-Roll,' added Juicy Lucy, well known for her legendary lubricity, even after taking on a whole company of eager teenaged SS men. 'No fuckee, no feedee!'

'Dead Right,' Split-Beaver and the rest joined in angrily, faces red with indignation. 'What else *can* we do, but lie on our backs and spread 'em!'

Otto had been adamant. That very night he had closed the doors of the '1st Mobile Brothel (Other Ranks Only)' for the last time and had set off with the Count and Deep Throat, who had remained strangely silent during the row that had erupted after his announcement of the afternoon. Of course, she had already known that she was the only one of the whores Otto had planned to take with him.

'Why,' Otto had declared excitedly to the Count when he had objected, 'that girl has got class. Your common, ordinary stubble-hopper has no appreciation of the kind of frog-piggery that girl can get up to. She's more your officer-and-gent type. Why she could swallow a bayonet sideways that one! Capital on the hoof, as it were. 'Cos the Amis like that sort of thing, as you well know, Count. How the Amis ever have kids, I don't know. They never seem to want to stick their salami in the right place. All they seem to know is heads down – and Deep Throat is just the girl for that sort of piggery!'

That had been two weeks ago. Now, thanks to Deep Throat and her permanent lover, Staff Sergeant Elmer P.

Rocock (known to all behind his back as 'raw cock'), they were safely installed as loyal workers for the Red Ball Express and wholesale purveyors of Camels and Chesterfields to the black markets of Aachen, Dueren, Juelich and surrounding districts.

'It is the best of all worlds,' Otto had attempted to convince the Count more than once. 'Honest physical labour in the open air, working for the cause of freedom and democracy, with a nice safe business arrangement on the side, with dear loyal Deep Throat as our insurance policy against any unpleasant surprises . . . *Why, we've made it at last, Count*!'

But the Count had remained obstinately dissatisfied and, as had been the case so often in the past, Otto Stahl, who had been attempting – and failing – to run away from Hitler's war ever since September 1939 was proved wrong. In this March of 1945, as the Western Allies prepared to make their great assault crossing against Germany's last natural bastion, the Rhine, Fate was still against Frau Stahl's handsome son. The war was not yet to release him . . .

'*Nomen es omen*, eh,' the hearty American voice boomed. 'Steel by name – and steel by nature!'[1]

Otto froze, C ration case in his hands, a cold finger of fear tracing its way down his spine. How often had that shitty Latin tag, always accompanied by a hearty, knowing laugh such as the one he had just heard, heralded trouble – serious trouble – for himself and the Count. Wearily, very wearily, like a condemned man waiting to hear his sentence, he turned to face the speaker.

He was a big, hearty man, who looked as if he might have high blood pressure, with one of those 'glad-hander' American faces, save that his eyes remained perfectly cold; and he was wearing the golden sphinx badge of the CIC[2] on his collar.

[1] *Stahl* is the German word for 'steel'.
[2] Counter-Intelligence Corps.

Otto's heart sank as he recognized the US colonel's insignia, but the Count's face lit up and he whispered out of the side of his mouth, 'The Great Game, Otto, we are being asked to take part in the Great Game once more. Adventure beckons yet again!'

Otto did not even have the heart to curse. Numbly he accepted his fate as the American boomed, 'My word, gentlemen, what a pleasure it is to meet two famed experts such as yourselves!' He stretched out a hand like a steam shovel and grabbed the Count's dainty, well-manicured hand. 'Sir, it is a real honour to shake the hand of the legendary Count von der Weide himself, alias Dr Rantzau, alias William B. Harper, Mynheer van Elst, alias Monsieur Le Comte de deux Eglises, Semor Angelo, Xavier de Dos Santos . . .' He winked solemnly. 'Yessir, we know all about your outstanding record.' He turned on Otto and crushed his hand so firmly the other man winced. 'And you, too, Otto. My God, your memoirs will be worth a fortune after the war, I do declare.'

Otto tugged his hand free and muttered under his breath, 'Shit on the shingle, I couldn't write my own frigging name – *now*!'

The American didn't seem to hear. Instead he said, 'But, I'm being impolite. Let me introduce myself. I am Colonel Al E. Ersenbrick, the Third.' He grinned at them hugely, though those cunning brown eyes of his still did not light. 'Just call me Al for short. Swell job you guys did for us in North Africa and Sicily in forty-three. That's why I am here in person, guys.'[1]

'So, you want us for the Great Game again, eh . . . er, Al?' the Count asked eagerly, his eyes gleaming suddenly.

Dramatically, the American held up his finger to his lips. 'Shush, Count, even here the walls have ears. But you are not far wrong.'

The Count beamed at Otto. 'Did you hear that, my boy. High adventure once more, after all this humdrum business. *High adventure*!'

'Yes indeedy!' Colonel Ersenbrick, the Third echoed.

[1] See *Otto and the Yanks* for further details.

'But we cannot discuss the matter here.' He turned to Staff Sergeant Rocock, who stood there, bent shouldered, blank-eyed, and wilting, drained of his life fluid by the cunning mouth of Deep Throat, known among the NCOs' command as the 'Dracula of Dueren'. 'Take us to the safe-room, Sergeant. There are spies everywhere. We can trust no one any more.' He looked severely at the utterly weary NCO, as if he half-suspected him, too. 'Move it, soldier!' he commanded.

'Yessir, Colonel sir,' the NCO answered wearily. 'Please follow me, sir.' Sergeant Rocock stumbled off, shoulders hunched with utter fatigue, as the Count clapped his pudgy hands in absolute delight and followed him eagerly.

Otto groaned and, like a condemned man, went after them. It was starting all over again . . .

At the other side of the barracks, the little hook-nosed American with a captain's silver bars and the screaming eagle insignia of the US 101st Airborne Division on his arm, lowered his binoculars thoughtfully. 'Hairy Prick' had asked him to observe the two Krauts and report his findings afterwards. Well, for his money, they looked like cannonfodder, pure and simple. That kinda Kraut came a dime-a-dozen, doomed for the big chop right from the very start. He shrugged and dismissed them from his thoughts. He wasn't going with them on their mission, that was for sure, and it was a very comforting thought.

Captain Moishe MacTavish took a cigarette out of his pocket and lit it with all the deliberation and thoroughness of a man at ease with the world, who had no pressing engagements this side of 1945.

'You jig-jig, soldier?' a voice asked.

Moishe turned slowly. 'Baby, I jig-jig, zig-zag, and . . .' he stopped short suddenly.

Garrison cycle was standing there simpering at him, her short dress raised yet once again, invitingly.

'Oh, my God!' he gasped. 'Put that goddam rug away, willya, baby!'

'Is for nozin,' she persisted.

'Hide the frigging carpet, willya!' he snapped.

'*Nozin.*' Garrison cycle tried one last time.

But the sharp-faced little man with the hook of a nose was not to be tempted. 'Nozin is for nozin in this world, baby,' he said with the air of a man who knew, slumping back in his seat and beginning to puff reflectively at his Camel. Now, old 'Hairy Prick' would be giving them the spiel, he told himself, the poor Kraut cruds.

'Fag,' Garrison cycle said angrily, lowering her skirt. 'Goddam fag!'

But Captain Moishe MacTavish was not listening. For he was back in that wonderful dream world of his, with the white coral sand, waving palm trees and plenty of dusky maidens in grass skirts – where there was no goddam war!

THREE

'*Werewolf*,' Colonel Ersenbrick snapped. 'That's the name of the game.'

Outside the little room, the radio blasted out Glenn Miller's 'American Patrol' and an exhausted Rocock stumbled from shower to shower, turning them on so that the running water would drown out anything said in the room.

Otto and the Count looked blank and the American said hastily, 'Don't it mean anything to you, gentlemen?'

Otto shook his head and the Count ventured, 'A medieval legend about the ability of some men to transform themselves into wolves at certain . . .'

'We're talking about the here and now, Count,' Ersenbrick barked irritatedly, 'about March, nineteen hundred and *frigging* forty-five! Not about fifteen hundred and *frigging* forty-five.' Obviously Colonel Ersenbrick was an angry man, who suppressed his rage by an effort of sheer willpower.

'Could you perhaps enlighten us, sir?' the Count asked as, outside, Rocock's weary voice boomed in the hollow confines of the shower room.

'Oh, not now, *schnuggi . . . please*!'

Otto smiled to himself. It would be Deep Throat. She just couldn't leave the poor harassed American alone. They said he had bought the PX out of Johnson's Baby Oil in order to soothe his very sensitive member. No wonder, given the Dracula of Dueren's insatiable thirst.

'Yes, of course, Count. Forgive me. These people are getting on my goddam nerves and the top brass are breathing down my back to get something done about it. Well, then, here goes. Last November, when it became clear to the wheels in Nazi Germany that they were going to lose the war, it was decided to set up an underground organization like the Polacks and the Frogs have had throughout the Occupation. For the most part, the recruits to this underground organization were to be drawn from those fanatical kids of the Hitler Youth, girls as well as boys, by the way. Okay, so the Krauts set the thing up, called it Operation Werewolf – yeah, that's where the name came from – recruited five thousand odd kids, who were trained specialists in demolition, sabotage, clandestine warfare and the like – and *nothing* happened! Indeed, our own Intelligence had completely forgotten about the Werewolves until this month. We had other things to do.' He paused significantly and the Count leaned forward, mouth hanging open like a village idiot, dark eyes gleaming excitedly, waiting for the big, bluff American colonel's next revelation. For his part, Otto tensed, feeling the well known twinge of fear and apprehension. They were being talked into something again, something very, very dangerous. He knew it with the instant clarity of a vision. He waited.

'But this March, things started to happen. First these little bastards killed *Oberbuergermeister* Oppenhoff of Aachen. Six of them, including a girl and a sixteen year old kid, murdered him on his own doorstep and escaped safely. Thereafter they started murdering or threatening officials appointed by the Military Government throughout the Rhineland and yesterday they did this.' Like a conjuror producing a rabbit out of a top-hat, he whipped two poor quality photographs out of his Ike blouse and held them up for the two friends to see. The Count gasped. One showed a fat man slumped on a doorstep, his face a mass of congealed blood, only the eyes giving it any semblance of human form. The other showed a garden gate. On it a Z-shaped mark had been hurriedly carved.

'The Mayor of Juelich, assassinated by the little buggers,' Ersenbrick said through gritted teeth, a nerve ticking electrically at the side of his face. 'And there you see the sign of the Werewolf – the *Wolfsangel*, I believe you call it in German.'

'The wolf-iron!' the Count breathed, impressed. 'My

God, it's like in the deepest Middle Ages. Ritual killing and the mark of the avenger!'

Ersenbrick nodded grimly. 'And you can just imagine the impression these strange killings are having on the local civilians. They're a superstitious lot at the best of times. Since these events occurred they are refusing to co-operate with the American Military Government in case it happens to them, and with this big Rhine op about to take place any day now, we can't afford to have trouble in the rear areas. Ike is worried, I can tell you, gentlemen[1], real damned worried.'

'How sad for the general!' Otto sneered.

But the American wasn't listening. Neither was the Count. The latter hung on the colonel's every word, eyes gleaming with anticipation. 'Not only is Ike worried about our rear areas,' Ersenbrick continued, 'he is also concerned about the Alpine Fortress and what a combination of Werewolves and fanatical SS troops might achieve up there.'

'Alpine Fortress?' the Count queried.

'The Alps of Bavaria and Austria. We have had confirmed reports that the Nazis have built some kind of last ditch fortifications down there and are withdrawing most of their crack SS divisions from the Russian front to join them. Imagine that combination – SS toughs dug in in the mountains and these bands of murdering schoolkids everywhere behind our lines. Christ, the war in Germany could continue for ever!' Suddenly Colonel Ersenbrick looked a very unhappy and harassed man. 'And I'm gonna be voted on the Democrat ticket for Congress soon. My whole goddam political career could still be ruined by this goddam war.' He took out a large flowered silk handkerchief and mopped the sweat from his furrowed brow.

Outside, Rocock was bellowing helplessly above the roar of the showers and the brassy blast of Glenn Miller, 'For crying out loud, *schatzi*, willya get yer hand off'n my flies!'

Suddenly Ersenbrick hammered his fist down on the table so that both the Count and Otto jumped. 'So,

[1] Ike: Eisenhower, Supreme Allied Commander.

gentlemen,' he declared like a man who had just made up his mind to indulge in some dramatic action, 'the little buggers must be stopped. But how?' He answered his own question. 'There are too many of the short-pants bastards to take out individually, of course. Christ, we'd have to arrest every frigging Kraut schoolkid in the country as a Werewolf suspect! No, gentlemen, that's not the way to do it. We've got to rip off the head and kill the monster that way.' He made a gesture with his big pudgy hands, as if he were twisting the neck of some unfortunate chicken. 'And who is that head, the master-mind behind the whole frigging operation? I shall tell you. It's *Reichsführer* Heinrich Himmler, head of the SS. Take him out and the whole thing collapses on the spot!' Suddenly he beamed at his two listeners, as if he were very pleased with himself.

Carefully, very carefully, already half-knowing the answer even before he posed his question, Otto asked, 'But where is Himmler, Colonel? . . . And how . . . how are you going to . . . er . . . take him out?'

'Good question, son,' Ersenbrick said heartily. 'Glad you asked it.'

Otto's heart sank. Here it came.

'We know exactly where Himmler will be in three days' time from now. He will be at Wewelsberg Castle south of Brunswick. How do we know? I'll tell you. Because for the last ten years he has always gone to the castle on this day to meet the rest of the SS high-ups. You see, they've got some sort of nutty secret society going up there among themselves – kinda like the freemasons.' Hurriedly he twisted the big black ring on his little finger and added, 'Don't get me wrong, fellas. That's nothing against the masons. I'm one myself. Anyway, they meet annually up there and start rapping the tables and all that kinda mumbo-jumbo. Shake the bones, Sambo sort of thing. He's never missed a meeting right throughout the war, and we're pretty damned sure he won't miss this one, especially as it looks as if it's gonna be their last get-together.'

He let them absorb the information. Outside in the

shower-room, Rocock was pleading in a cracked, desperate voice, 'But *schnuggi*, I'm plumb worn out. Drained . . . drained of every last drop. Honest, at this moment, I ain't got enough spit to wet my lips!'

'So, guys, we know where he is,' Ersenbrick continued. 'The problem is how are we gonna take him out? We've considered a para-attack. But apparently all the paras are needed by Monty for his attack on the Rhine. We've considered an armoured thrust by the US First Army towards the castle. But it turns out the goddam place is right in the middle of the SS's own armoured training school. So,' he shrugged, frowning suddenly, 'that leaves the fly-boys of the 8th US Air Force in England.'

Otto's heart jumped with relief. So they were not going to be dragged into the nasty business with Himmler after all. He had seen pictures of that pasty-faced little cop with his clerk's pince-nez often enough in the past and he did not look the kind of man Frau Stahl's handsome son would like to tangle with. He had that constipated look that all the most evil villains always wore.

'There's only one problem with those fly-boys,' Ersenbrick went on. 'Most of them couldn't piss in a bucket! They are the world's worst bombers. Only yesterday they were sent out to bomb Cologne – and what did they do? They bombed our own guys at Aachen! No wonder the dogfaces call them the American *Luftwaffe*. And that in broad daylight with the sun shining.' He shook his head in mock wonder. Otto closed his eyes tightly. He fervently wished he could press his hands over his ears like a frightened child, trying to blot out a nightmare; for he knew now what was to come. It did.

'So, fellas, what are we gonna do? This. We're gonna have some reliable Joes on the ground guiding those big bacon-and-egg hotshots from Limeyland right to the target, so that they can't frigging well miss.'

The Count straightened up, eyes gleaming, chest thrown out proudly. 'You mean, Colonel,' he cried fervently, 'you want us to volunteer to be those guides?'

'Exactly, Count, exactly. Hot shit, you're real professionals. You know the score right off. No need to draw you two guys a picture.' He beamed at Count von der Weide and wondered why the younger one had suddenly screwed up his eyes. Perhaps he was overcome with emotion at this sudden honour which was being bestowed upon him?

'Did you hear that, Otto?' the Count cried. 'We're back in the Great Game! We have a mission! At last there is something exciting happening again.'

'Yer,' Otto said in a hollow voice, opening his eyes once more, 'like having yer stupid turnip blown off by an SS man – or,' he indicated Colonel Ersenbrick, who was beaming encouragingly at the Count, 'by one of those Ami flyboys who can't even piss in a bucket.'

But Count von der Weide was no longer listening. Already he was going into one of his postures: a tragic but romantic figure, the man of destiny, who would, if needs be, sacrifice his own life to save Germany.

Outside in the showers, Staff Sergeant Elmer P. Rocock was crying desperately in a cracked voice, obviously at the end of his tether, 'No, *schnuggi*, no! For God's sake, have mercy on me, baby . . . Can't yer see I'm on duty. No, *schnuggi*, please. *Get your teeth off 'n it* . . .'

FOUR

It drizzled miserably.

Up ahead in no-man's-land a wrecked tank lay in the field, one track stretched out behind it like a shattered limb. To the right, a group of cows caught in yesterday's shellfire lay dead and bloated, their legs sticking straight upwards. Everywhere there were shell-holes fresh, brown and steaming like the work of giant moles. A long way off to the east, the heavy guns continued to thunder, and every now and again the grey dripping sky was ripped apart by a flash of violent light.

'Okay,' said the big rangy infantry captain, crouching next to Otto and the Count in the damp ditch, the rain dropping from his helmet like grey tears, 'this is the drill. The Krauts are in those houses to left and right of the road. They ain't done much for the last twenty-four hours 'cept scratch their Kraut asses. But they're there all right.'

The Count frowned at such crudity, but by now he was used to the Americans. He said nothing.

'Once we go in, all hell is gonna be let loose. You can bet your sweet ass on that.' The tall captain talked slowly, with long, significant pauses, as if he was very tired or used to talking to idiots, or perhaps both.

Miserably, Otto, dressed in the grey uniform of a *Hauptsturmbannführer*, complete with a chestful of decorations, listened as the American briefed them and stared at the Ami infantrymen all round him in the ditch. They all seemed very old or incredibly young. But all were dirty, unshaven and laden down with every conceivable weapon of destruction. Knives, clubs, rocket launchers, mortars, rifles, sub-machines – everything. They were walking arsenals, constantly spitting and gesturing, the loud-mouthed reinforcements watched in cynical silence by the handful of bearded dirty veterans.

'Okay,' the captain started again, as a flight of rockets howled into the grey sky, trailing white smoke and angry, fiery sparks behind them, 'we hit them at dusk. We go in fast. And we come out even faster, you'd better believe it, mister. With them shitheels they're sending up these days from battalion, it's the only way. Jesus H. Christ, they all think they're frigging John Wayne till the frigging shit hits the fan! Look at 'em, willya.'

Otto and the Count turned and followed the direction of his disgusted gaze. The effect of that sudden rocket salvo was all too obvious. As far as the eye could see, the suddenly ashen-faced replacements were unbuttoning their flies and urinating rapidly along the ditch, while the veterans guffawed with delight.

'First sign. They'll piss and piss, until the Krauts knock the piss outa 'em for good,' the captain commented. He laughed coarsely and dismissed the frightened young soldiers with a wave of his dirty paw.

Suddenly Otto realized that the American captain was tired, very tired; his reflexes were shot. He had dead man written all over his face. He wouldn't survive the rest of the war.

'Okay, while the John Waynes are shooting up the Krauts, you two guys,' he continued, 'take to those woods at three o'clock. See 'em?'

They nodded in unison.

'Intelligence says there are no Krauts in them. But what do those frigging fairies of Intelligence know. There could be half the frigging Kraut army in there.'

'You mean it could be defended?' Otto asked hesitantly.

'Sure,' the captain answered with an easy shrug. Somewhere a heavy machine-gun had begun to chatter ponderously like an irate elderly woodpecker. Red and green flares began to soar into the grey dripping gloom above the German-held village. The overture had commenced. Soon the opera would begin.

'Sure, at least they could have fixed-fire machine-guns covering the firebreaks. There'll be mines too. Booby-traps. The Krauts are great at booby-traps. They know what shitheels your average dogfaces are. They'd pick up a piece of monkey shit for a souvenir if it was laying there.' He spat contemptuously. 'Frigging Krauts – too frigging efficient. Wish they'd frigging realize that they've lost the frigging war and frigging well give up like frigging Ike sez. Instead of frigging . . .'

He never finished his lament. With startling suddenness, there was a heavy, asthmatic crump. Otto ducked instinctively, as did most of the soldiers. With a baleful howl the first salvo of shells whizzed over their shoulders. 'Outgoing mail!' one of the reinforcements yelled exuberantly.

'Frig off, John Wayne!' the captain cried contemptuously, as the shells slammed into the houses up the road. They shimmied and shivered wildly like a stage backdrop and then disappeared into a thick cloud of yellow smoke, tinged here and there by cherry-red flames.

The captain fastened his helmet strap and clutched his carbine in his right hand as a fresh salvo hurtled above their heads with a banshee-like howl. 'On yer frigging feet!' he yelled, and rose, glaring at the men crouched there.

At the other end of the ditch, the top sergeant shrilled red-faced on his whistle. Reluctantly the bearded veterans rose to their feet. The reinforcements hesitated. The top sergeant didn't. He aimed a tremendous kick at the nearest ashen-faced youth. 'All right, you frigging canteen commandos,' he snarled. 'Off yer frigging keesters. Move it, you frigging heroes.' He swung his tommy-gun round on them, as if he might well use it on the reluctant soldiers if they didn't.

Slowly they rose to their feet, most of them trembling visibly, as the barrage mounted in ever-increasing fury, making the very earth tremble beneath their feet. Up ahead, red and green signal flares were shooting into the dripping sky, sounding their urgent warnings to the Germans further back.

The captain stuck out a dirty hand. Otto took it. The American had death written all over his haggard, worn face. 'Best of luck, you guys.' He gave them a wry grin,

'And if you do meet that frigging house-painter, A-dolf, willya please tell him to stop this frigging shit. It's getting awful frigging dangerous!'

Then he was gone at the head of his men: a line of infantry plodding slowly across the sodden fields towards the burning village, rifles held across their chests, shoulders hunched, like weary farmers coming home after a long day's hard toil. In front of them there came the first vicious hiss of a Spandau. The Germans were waiting for them.

Otto gave the Americans a last sad look. He felt sorry for them. Some of them – perhaps all of them – would not see the end of this grey March day. And for what? He shook his head.

A sudden burst of bullets ripped the length of the road in front of them in high-pitched fury, throwing up angry little blue eruptions of sparks and tar. Otto waited no longer. 'Come on, Count,' he cried above the racket. He grabbed the older man's hand. 'Let's go!'

Holding hands, they ran like two excited schoolboys suddenly released from school towards the woods . . .

Now to their left, a fierce fire-fight had broken out. Spurts of vicious red flame stabbed the grey smoke-fog. Machine-guns chattered angrily. There were cries, moans of agony, commands; and always over and over again, that desperate plea in both English and German: '*Medic . . . for Chrissake, medic, where are you . . .*?' and '*Sanitater . . . Hilfe . . . Sanitater . . . ich bin verwundet . . .*'

At one point a man had reeled past them through the firs, whether German or American, they had not been able to tell, his face a black shattered mask through which the eyes glowed a mad-white, holding up his hands for mercy, limbs twitching and trembling as if he were in the grip of some terrible tropical fever. They had heard him thrashing his way through the trees until he had vanished, leaving them crouched there, hearts thumping like crazy trip-hammers. But now the sounds of battle were becoming muted by the thick ranks of rain-heavy, dripping green firs. Otto and the Count sweated as they worked their way through the trees, bodies tensed, eyes narrowed to slits, trying to pierce the green gloom for the first sign of danger, ears alert for any sound that could indicate sudden, violent death.

The wood had been recently occupied. That was clear enough. There were empty ration cans everywhere in the undergrowth, rusting barbed wire, and close to the foxholes lay grenades and belts of machine-gun ammunition, which seemed to have been abandoned in a great hurry.

'According to the map, Otto,' the Count wheezed, as they skirted yet another line of foxholes among the trees, 'once we get through the wood, there is about one kilometre to go down the road to the hamlet of Galenhausen.'

Otto nodded.

'And you can imagine, it will be guarded. After all, it is only about three kilometres behind the front line. There'll be at least a unit of base stallions there, if nothing else.'

'Yes,' Otto said grimly, 'and let's hope that those Ami forged documents we have are all up to scratch. If our ID isn't right, they won't play games with us for long. In zero-comma-nothing seconds, it'll be the nearest telephone mast for us and we'll be dancing a nice shitting little jig – at the end of two metres of rope!'

The Count swallowed hard, and clutched at his collar, as if it had suddenly become too tight for him. 'Please, don't even *think* things like that, Otto, my boy. It is too terrible to contemplate. But never fear, Otto, our American friends are terribly efficient, you know. It's the New World outlook and all that. The documents will be in perfect order, you'll see.'

'Oh go and stick yer salami up yer own arse,' Otto snorted coarsely, irritated, as always, by the Count's unreasoning optimism, 'and give yersen a shitting cheap thrill! *Terribly efficient, my aching arse!*' He shook his head like a man sorely tried by this world and plodded on, shoulders hunched against the rain. Behind them, the sounds of battle began to grow ever fainter.

The Count tut-tutted at such coarseness. But, dutifully enough, he followed behind the younger man.

Just when they had almost reached the edge of the wood and were preparing to tackle the next obstacle – the road – the frightened voice startled them with its 'Hello, gentlemen . . . excuse me, please.' They swung round as one, pistols gripped in suddenly damp hands, hearts thumping away painfully.

A dark, fat shape in the grey of the Wehrmacht was standing there in the undergrowth, rifle clasped to the side in the position of attention.

'What in three devils' name,' Otto began, but he never finished.

The fat soldier quavered, the relief in his voice all too obvious. 'It's all right, boys, we're saved. The gentlemen are from the SS. They'll see we're well looked after now.' He gave a heart-felt sigh of relief as, all around him, scores of helmeted figures began to rise from the undergrowth like green ghosts from the grave.

Otto's mouth dropped open stupidly like that of a stranded cod. They had walked straight into the positions of what looked to him like a whole shitting company of infantry. In the growing darkness, he could see they were everywhere – and all were heavily armed. 'What . . . what's going on?' he stuttered, finding his voice at last, as the soldiers started to shuffle towards the surprised running-mates, as if it gave them a sense of security to be crowded together thus in the dripping dark wood. 'What are you lot doing here?' Suddenly Otto put iron into his voice, as he remembered his role, that of a tough, arrogant front-swine from the SS. 'Well, man, cat got your tongue! Speak up, will you?'

The fat soldier, who wore sergeant's stars on his collar, swallowed hard and replied, 'It was our CO, sir . . . I mean, *Hauptsturmführer* . . . When the Amis started shooting back there, he said he'd better go back to HQ at Galenhausen and check with the general . . . And then, sir, the second-in-command thought – when the CO didn't come back – he ought to see what had happened to the CO when he didn't return after half an hour . . . and the two young officer-cadets volunteered to accompany him as a sort of a bodyguard . . . and they left me in charge.' He stumbled to an awkward halt. 'That's how it was.'

Otto breathed a sigh of relief, and realized they had been damned lucky. If the company's officers hadn't beaten it, they might well be asking him and the Count some very unpleasant questions at this very moment. Out loud, he said, voice full of contempt, 'You mean, Sergeant, your officers have gone and done a bunk, the treacherous swine!' He thrust his pistol violently back into its holster. 'My God, I could castrate that kind of pig personally – *with a blunt razor blade*!'

The NCO trembled visibly and, instinctively, his free hand fell to his crotch, as if he feared that terrible fate might be his, if he weren't careful; the SS were very unpredictable. 'I don't know about that, sir . . . er, *Hauptsturmführer*. I'm just a simple soldier. All I know is that me and the boys are happy, damned happy, to see you.' There was a chorus of hoarse agreement from the others. 'Officers and gentlemen like you, and SS to boot, will know what to do with us,' he added cheerfully.

'Yes, I know what to do with you,' Otto said grimly to himself, 'drop the whole awkward bunch of you in the deepest shithouse I can find.'

But, at his side, the Count, falling automatically into his new role as an arrogant, cocky, tough SS officer, cried: 'Don't you worry, Sergeant. We will soon sort out this little mess. Worse things at sea, you know. *Gut*. Now listen to me and do exactly as I command.'

Otto groaned. They had hardly started on their mission, were not even through the front line, not to mention the dangers that lay ahead of them on the long way to Himmler's mysterious Wewelsberg Castle, and here they were, landed with over a hundred thick-skulled stubble-hoppers, with nowhere to go, but with them. The Count was talking to them as if he was personally going to lead them on a great counter-attack that would throw the whole Allied army back into the Channel. '*Mensch, das ist zum Kotzen!*' he fumed, telling himself, with that old familiar sinking feeling, that he and the Count were up to their hooters in shit once again, and that that old fart, the Count, did not even have the sense to keep his mouth shut!

FIVE

The general was a leather-faced old fart, who affected a monocle and looked suitably martially stern, as befitted a general. Every time he moved, he creaked slightly, as if most of his body was the product of spare-part surgery – leather, wood, metal and plastic. He was definitely the kind, Otto told himself wearily, who would fight to the last.

'The Americans got a bloody nose up there,' he now rasped and, taking off his wooden hand, slammed it on the kitchen table of the farmhouse which served as his divisional headquarters, as if to emphasize the point. 'Typical Yankee attack. Lots of artillery fire. But no infantry dash. Seems those stubble-hoppers of General Eisenhower's don't want to die. Can't understand it. Fellers not wanting to die a hero's death, what? Wouldn't tolerate it in the Wehrmacht, eh, gentlemen.' He slapped the table again with a snort of disgust and the candle flickered madly, throwing gigantic, wavering shadows on the wall.

Otto flashed the Count an anxious look. They had obviously fallen in with a typical military fire-eater – all guts and no brains. But the Count had, as always, slipped effortlessly into his new role. Now he was the typical SS officer, with his cap set at a rakishly daring angle, jaw thrust aggressively forward, an amused, if contemptuous, look set on his face, as he toyed with his pistol. Inwardly, Otto groaned. Why in heaven's name did he always land in such messes? Why hadn't the fat sergeant, standing outside with his company shuffling their feet impatiently like so many horses waiting to be off (and Otto knew in which direction), had the sense to run away like his officers had done? Why was fate always against Frau Stahl's handsome son when he tried so damned hard to avoid danger and the shitting war? Five long years he had worked his butt off in an attempt to escape – and here he was in March 1945 with the Allies already on the Rhine still fighting for shitting Adolf Hitler, the Greatest Captain of All Times, he didn't think? It was not shitting fair.

'So what will they do now?' the ancient general barked. He answered his own question, idly taking out his left eye and polishing it with his lapel before replacing it in the empty socket. 'They'll hit my left flank. And if they don't succeed there, they'll strike my right. Very elementary tactics. But no matter. As long as I have such stout fellows as you,' he nodded at a proud Count, 'we'll hold them till hell freezes over, what!'

The Count snapped to attention, gave a half-bow, and touched his gloved hand to the rim of his cap – like the bleeding head waiter at the Adlon Hotel, Otto could not help thinking, face set in a mask of worry and disgust. 'Sir, you need only give the command, and it will be the last bullet and the last man, *sir*!'

The old fart beamed. 'Well said, *Hauptsturm*, well said indeed!' he exclaimed with such enthusiasm that his false teeth nearly shot out from between his ancient lips. 'We will win this war yet, with officers like you!'

'It will be a pleasure to die for the holy cause of Germany, sir,' the Count answered piously.

Otto farted very impiously, but neither of the two old farts noticed; they were too busy having a patriotic love affair.

'Now then,' the general continued, 'let us discuss how I may employ your brave fellows who have . . .'

The rest of the general's words were drowned by a sudden roar, the clatter of metal, the grinding of steel wheels, as something came thundering down the slope outside at a tremendous rate, scattering the waiting soldiers to both sides with a strange whirring sound that was somehow oddly familiar to a bemused Otto.

'*Volle Deckung*!' the general shrieked and flung himself to the floor, his left leg sticking up in the air, as he did so, so that Otto, who tumbled after him, presumed he had a wooden leg, too. '*DUCK*!'

Next moment there was a huge explosion. The walls of the farmhouse seemed to bulge inwards and plaster trickled from the roof in a thick white rain. A wave of blast swept the door open. Otto felt the very air sucked from his lungs, leaving him choking and gasping for breath, as his unbelieving eyes took in the sight of a tram racing up into the air, its steel wheels whirling madly, in a spout of bright red flame. Next moment the door slammed shut once more, blocking out that impossible scene, and Otto was shaking his head like a boxer attempting to come out of a near knock-out.

For what seemed a long time, nobody moved, until finally the general rose in a complicated manner, accompanied by a series of alarming squeaks and groans, as if the blast had seriously affected the various artificial parts that made up his body. He sat down again, wiped his brow and snapped, 'Shitting trams . . . Wiped out my personal thunderbox at seventeen hundred hours yesterday. Imagine that. A chap's thunderbox! Is there nothing sacred?' He mopped his damp forehead again. 'What fiends those Americans must be. Not the kind of warfare one would expect from a European, what?' He glared fiercely at the two friends, who stared back at him in open-mouthed amazement.

'Did you say – trams, sir?' Otto asked finally, wiping the dust from his face.

'Yes, I did, *trams*. I've been attacked by some weapons in my time,' the general snorted. 'I remember back in the trenches, the Tommies once used their mortars to lob jam-jars filled with – er – ordure at us. But then they were those Tommies who wear skirts. Not real gentlemen. But even they never descended to such depths. *Trams*!'

'Did you really say trams, sir?' Otto repeated his question incredulously.

'I did! The Yankees have captured the old tram depot further up the hill out there. They load the damned trams with bombs, petrol, set them running down the slope without a driver. Naturally, they can't take the corner out there, come off the rails, and go careering all over the place.' He took his hand off again and slammed the wooden knuckles down on the table angrily. 'That kind of weapon should be banned. It's not legal. It does not differentiate between an ordinary stubble-hopper and an officer like myself. Absolutely inhumane!'

Outside Otto could hear his reluctant heroes reassembling and the fat fool of a sergeant shouting, 'Fall in, you lot. Come on, let's be having it! Remember you're with the SS now, you shower . . . Move it!'

Inwardly, Otto groaned. Was he going to be surrounded by fools and candidates for sudden death all his life? Was there going to be no end to this whole bloody business? He stopped short. The general was staring at the Count and him thoughtfully with his own bloodshot eye, lips pursed, as if he were considering something. As yet another tram came rattling down the tracks towards the bend, the general said hastily, 'I know it's no use offering two chaps like yourselves any tin[1]. You've got it all, the whole set, brave fellows that you are. But what about a week's leave in Berlin, all found, in a good hotel, plenty of bubble and a couple of rather excellent fillies over whom I've cocked my leg a few times in the past?'

'*For what*?' Otto shrieked as the tram rattled closer, bearing its cargo of death.

'Jolly good rides,' the general continued. 'These days I'm too old to do anything but a slow canter. But two young fellows like yourselves will soon bring 'em up to the full gallop, what?'

'*But what do we have to do?*' Otto cried desperately, eyes popping out of his head, clutching at straws before it was too late.

'Take out that damned tram depot before it is too late!' the general yelled back, and flung himself dramatically to the floor as the tram rose off the rails at the bend and went sailing high into the air to explode in mad fury a moment later . . .

'I'm not damn well gonna do it!' Otto declared hotly, as

[1] Tin: decorations for bravery.

they marched at the head of the company up the dark road that led to the woods from which they would attack the tram depot. 'Sod that for a tale. Getting my turnip blown off just to stop some Amis playing with a bunch of outsize toys!'

'But Otto,' the Count protested, still deep in his new role, 'the Fatherland is watching us. Think of the honour of the SS!'

'Count,' Otto tried to control his rising temper, 'you really are a silly old fart. We are working for the Amis. The sooner they end the war, the better it will be for Germany. We don't want to do anything that will make the war last a day longer than necessary. Got it?'

Suddenly the Count's new historic posture collapsed. He stopped and would have stood there in the path of the marching company, if Otto had not given him a sharp dig in the ribs and hissed, 'Keep on!'

'I understand completely, Otto,' the Count whispered as he stumbled on. 'But how are we going to get out of this mess? You know what they do when there's an attack on these days? They post chaindogs with machine-guns to the rear. Anybody who deserts the firing line gets a bullet through his brains for his pains.'

Otto nodded gloomily. He knew it well. In this terrible March, the only thing that kept most of the poor frightened downtrodden soldiers in the front line was the fear of sudden death at the hands of the military policemen, the chaindogs.

'I mean the two of us might make it,' the Count continued miserably. 'But how do we get rid of a company of infantrymen in the middle of the night?'

'I know, I know,' Otto snapped desperately, watching with alarm as the sky in front of him started to flicker with pink lights. The American artillerymen were already zeroing in on the German positions. It wouldn't be long before a full-scale artillery barrage descended upon this area. He knew the men behind him were as frightened as he was. They'd love nothing better than to hoof it right away. But this was the German army. You couldn't tell a

German soldier to hoof it smartish to the rear. The command was not included in their military vocabulary. Besides, there were still those damned chaindogs with their damned machine-guns. Otto's mind raced furiously as he attempted to find some way out of the mess they had found themselves in so unexpectedly, before it was too late.

Then he had it. It wasn't brilliant, but it was the only thing that came to mind at three o'clock on a cold March morning after a very, very hard day. '*Ein lied*,' he barked in his best SS officer's voice. '*Ein lied, Herr Feldwebel*!'

'A song, sir?' the fat sergeant behind him quavered. 'But sir, we're nearing the front line. The Amis will have a forward artillery observer up there somewhere. He'll report . . .'

'Damn the Ami FAO!' Otto snapped, hoping against hope that the Americans would indeed have an observer directing the artillery to the rear, hidden in the trees somewhere ahead of them – and that the Ami had damn sharp ears. He licked his suddenly parched lips. '*Eins, zwei, drei*,' he counted off the timing and burst next moment into '*O, du schoener Westerwald*!'

The years of unquestioning training paid off. As one, the weary infantrymen joined in. Lustily they bellowed out the old marching song as they came ever closer to the front line. Throwing out their chests as if these were still the great days when nothing could stop the Greater German Army, breath fogging the cold night air, their steel-shod boots stamping harshly on the cobbles, drowning out the rumble of the American guns.

'*Uber deine Wipfel weht der Wind so kalt . . . du schoener Westerwald . . .*' At the head of the singing men, Otto tensed, waiting for the first shriek, which would indicate the Ami forward artillery observer had spotted them and had radioed back to bring down fire on these stupid Krauts.

Nothing happened! The American guns remained obstinately silent in their sector, as the steam started to go out of the men and the road became ever steeper. Their singing began to falter. Desperately Otto cried, 'Let us give them the "Horst Wessel Song" and show the Ami swine who they are dealing with this night – the Armed SS . . . Now then, *eins, zwei, drei*!'

Wearily, but obediently, the soldiers burst into the bold marching song of the Nazi Party, the fat sergeant doing his best, gasping for breath like some ancient asthmatic in the throes of a fatal attack. '*Heute gehort uns Deutschland . . . und morgen die ganze Welt* . . .' Desperately, Otto bellowed out the hated Nazi song with all his strength, praying that the Americans would hear and a burst of artillery fire would end this mad adventure into the night. But that wasn't to be. The guns remained silent and, from somewhere up ahead in the darkness, a weary American voice cried plaintively in poor German, '*Nix singen, heinis . . . Amerikan soldats schlafen* . . . For crying out loud, will you stop that frigging singing! How the hell's a guy gonna get some frigging sleep with that racket going on . . .'

The singing faltered and suddenly the soldiers were slogging their way miserably up the hill in silence, heads bent like cattle being led to the slaughter.

Otto's heart sank. He had failed. At dawn they would have to attack that damned tram depot after all. At his side, the Count said cheerfully enough, 'Always like a bit of singing on the march. Puts heart into the men, don't you think, Otto?' He smiled winningly at his old running-mate.

Otto didn't reply; he couldn't. At that particular moment in time he could have cheerfully strangled his friend, with his own bare hands. They marched on.

SIX

Dawn came slowly, as if reluctant to shed light on this grim, war-torn world. Gradually the dark shadows began to flee from the wood and, to the east, the sky flushed a dirty white, outlining the ruined landscape, the shell-shattered trees standing out like giant toothpicks. Here and there a machine-gun still chattered and, far away towards the Rhine, the permanent barrage rumbled. Otherwise all was a heavy, brooding silence that seemed as ominous and threatening as the dawn itself.

Together with the Count, Otto crawled through the undergrowth, steadily approaching the sound of hammering, interrupted every now and again by a muted order in English. Up at the hilltop depot, the Amis were preparing yet another street-car for its fiery progress downhill towards the general's headquarters.

Otto parted the bushes in front of him – and gulped with shock. In the thin grey light, he could make out the ragged corpse hanging on the rusting barbed wire, arms outstretched, eyes gone where the crows had picked them out, like some latterday Christ on the cross.

At his side the Count heaved and fought back the hot vomit which flooded his throat. 'Oh, my God, Otto, is . . . is that a man?'

Otto nodded grimly. 'A man – American or German, it makes no difference. A man dead, killed violently for the New Order – or Democracy,' he added bitterly. 'What does it shitting well matter? The poor shit is very dead . . . Come on . . .'

They crawled on, past old shell-holes, the ground littered with cartridge cases, bodies of men caught in some counter-attack or other, American and German, the waxen-faced ghastly tableau of the violently done to death, clasping each other in the awesome finality of battle – and paper:

paper everywhere, as if someone had been commissioned specifically to strew the killing-ground with bits and pieces of it.

The sound of hammering was quite close now and Otto judged that they had come as far as they dared. He reasoned that if they were discovered in SS uniform by the Americans there would be no cosy prisoner-of-war camp for them with Red Cross parcels, camp concerts and correspondence courses to improve one's self. The Amis hated the SS. It would be the nearest wall and a quick burst of tommy-gun fire. 'Let's hold it here, Count,' he gasped and again parted the undergrowth.

They had crawled further than he had thought. The tram depot was below them and he could see the khaki-clad figures busy at their task of filling another battered yellow tram with high explosives, while the company comic, presumably, painted in black lettering on its side, '*Happy Birthday Adolf*' – '*Here's V-3 for You. Love, From the Boys*'. Further on, two hefty soldiers were switching the points on the rusting lines that led downhill with crowbars. Soon another damned tram would be sent hurtling down the slope towards the German lines.

Next to Otto, the Count said, 'There seems to be an awful lot of them, Otto, and they're pretty well armed, too. They've got machine-gun posts set up all over the place.' He indicated the sandbagged weapon pits that surrounded the depot with a dirty finger. 'In the attack, one needs a ratio of at least three to one to succeed and I'm afraid our company does not number more than a hundred. Our chances of a successful attack are slim, very slim, Otto, my dear boy.'

Otto glared at him. 'You know, Count,' he said, more in sadness than anger, 'I sometimes think you've got a little bird up there in your top storey which goes twit-twit. I've got no shitting intention of attacking 'em. Ain't there been enough poor stubble-hoppers on both sides killed already? We don't want to plant any more of them so that they can watch the taties grow from underneath. No sir!'

'But what are we going to do, Otto? We can't go back

without having made an attempt and we can't retreat . . . the chaindogs would shoot us down mercilessly.'

'Nor,' Otto rubbed it in grimly, 'can we go over to the Americans. You know that old Hairy Prick told us if we screwed up the mission, he'd have us in Leavenworth for the rest of our natural days – and then some. And I believe him. That one is ruthless.'

'So what alternative do we have, Otto?' the Count quavered. 'They – all of them – have got us, as you would put it in your own quaint working-class way, by the short and curlies.'

Before Otto could answer that question, a loud command echoed from the depot below. Almost immediately the tram the Americans had been working on started to move forward, a single soldier at the controls, twirling the brass handles, while his comrades gave three cheers, raising their helmets as if in parting salutation. Flames started to pour from the vehicle's broken windows. Already the first explosive bullets began to crack and splutter, spitting red and yellow flames like those of fireworks on New Year's Eve[1] to both flanks.

The tram started to gather speed. The man at the wheel kept to his post. The men with the crowbars threw the points. The tram rattled on, smoke belching from it in a thick black stream as it bucked and reared on the track. Now it was going up a small incline, losing speed a little. At the controls, the lone GI threw away his helmet and half-hung out of the cab, watching the track carefully. It had almost surmounted the incline. The driver hesitated. In a moment it would plunge over the rise and go hurtling down the hill towards the German positions below. The driver waited no longer. He flung himself out of the cab and hit the ground in a flurry of dust, rolling over and over, as the tram disappeared, driverless now, in a great whoosh and rattle of protesting metal.

Now the only sound was that of the tram racing down the tracks, out of sight but very much there. The waiting GIs clasped their hands tightly to their helmets. One or

[1] Germans sometimes celebrate New Year's Eve by letting off fireworks.

two thrust their fingers into their ears, shoulders hunched expectantly, like schoolkids waiting for the big bang at some firework display.

They didn't have to wait long. Suddenly the earth trembled. Bright red flame shot high into the air from below, followed an instant later by a thick, whirling black mushroom of smoke. Otto felt the blast strike him across the face like the blow from a flabby wet fist; and abruptly the GIs crowded around the tram depot were cheering, jumping up and down excitedly, slapping each other on the back heartily, as if congratulating one another.

A few minutes later they began to move back to the next tram and busy themselves once again, with barrels of tar, jerricans of petrol, cases of shells and the like, preparing yet another tram for that mad death-ride down the hill.

The Count frowned and looked at Otto crouching next to him. 'They seem to have an awful lot of the things left, my boy,' he said. 'I wonder how many of them they still have?'

Otto did not answer immediately. His handsome tough face was worried, his brow creased in a frown, as if he were thinking hard and not coming to any conclusion. 'A damned lot of 'em,' he said finally. 'Too many.'

'Then we'll have to attack the place,' the Count said miserably. 'I'm afraid a lot of those chaps back there will not survive the attack, Otto, my boy.'

The younger man shook his head. 'Nobody's gonna suffer on this one, Count,' he said firmly, his mind suddenly made up. 'There's been enough killing. There will be no more.'

'But what do you mean, Otto? How can it be done . . .?'

Otto had no time for answering questions. Instead, he grabbed the bewildered Count's elbow and guided him back into the cover of the bushes. 'Come on, Count, we've got a lot of work in front of us this morning. *Los*!'

'Dead ground,' Otto announced and straightened himself up to his full height. 'You're all right now, men. The Amis can't see you down here.'

Gratefully the infantrymen, laden down with their weapons as well as the heavy log that each of them was carrying on Otto's instructions, straightened up, too, and sighed with relief.

They were in a hollow, hidden from the Americans below in the depot, though they could hear them well enough, hammering and generally preparing another tram, alone save for a herd of cows lowing piteously to their right. They obviously hadn't been milked for some time for their udders hung almost to the wet grass, and they were in too much pain even to crop the lush fodder.

'Poor shits,' the fat sergeant said. 'I had a small farm up north before the war. Never could understand a farmer who would let his beasts suffer like that.'

Otto shrugged unsympathetically. He had always thought that people cared far too much about animals and not enough about their fellow human beings. 'The only udders I've ever worried about, Sergeant, is the ones that female gash carry around with them under their jumpers. Come on now, let's be getting on with it.'

In a narrow file, hugging the grass bank to their left, followed by the miserable mooing of the cows, they started to make their way towards the tramline that led down the hill. Otto could already hear the clatter of another monster as it commenced its downward descent, accompanied by the excited hoots and catcalls of the Americans. He stopped momentarily, ear cocked to the wind. Yes, there it was. The thing really was slowing down a trifle, as it took the little slope, before plunging downwards straight for the German lines.

'Look,' the fat sergeant gasped. '*Just look at the bugger!*'

A hundred metres away, the tram shot over the brow of the hill, trailing smoke and flames behind it, its sides bedaubed with swastikas and rude remarks, bucking and rearing down the track, wheels screeching in metallic protest as the fiery juggernaut hurtled towards the German lines. They tensed automatically as it disappeared beyond the trees, waiting for the explosion. A moment later it happened and they caught sight of a front bogie whirling round and round, high in the air above the smoke-topped firs, before it was overtaken by the sudden upthrust of blast and thick black smoke.

Otto sighed and shook his head. 'Great crap on the Christmas tree,' he cursed, 'what a shitting war . . .!' He shouldered his own log, taken from the huge pile that the foresters had conveniently arranged for them before the battle had reached this remote place, and trudged on. A little apprehensively, the others followed, wondering why the Amis had not dug in their infantry here to protect the depot beyond.

It was the Count, who, surprisingly enough (for most of the time he seemed oblivious to the real world, preferring to live in a dream world of his own), discovered the reason why. 'I say, Otto,' he called five minutes later, 'there seems to be some sort of a sign or warning over there . . . Look, on that piece of barbed wire.'

Otto followed the direction of his gaze and gasped with shock. In these last terrible years, fate had forced him onto the battlefield all too often. He had seen that same sign before in Africa, Sicily, Italy, Russia and France, but he had never managed to overcome that sense of shock, the feeling that his legs had abruptly been turned into India-rubber, whenever he had seen it: the black skull-and-crossbones on the yellow enamel plate with that awesome legend printed beneath it: '*ACHTUNG MINEN!*'

For one long moment, as the men behind him stumbled to a ragged halt, he simply stood there, unable to speak, until the Count asked, 'What's the matter, Otto . . . Anything wrong?'

'Wrong!' Otto exploded angrily and flung the heavy log to the wet ground. '*Everything's shitting wrong!*' He slammed his clenched fist against the nearest tree in anger and did not even feel the pain of the blow. 'What did you think, standing there like a wet fart waiting to hit the side of the thunderbox?'

'But I don't understand, Otto,' the Count exclaimed helplessly.

'It's a shitting minefield!' Otto exploded miserably. 'No wonder the Amis didn't dig in here in the dead ground! That silly old fart of a general down there with his plastic prick, has had a minefield laid up here . . . Christ on a crutch, what are we gonna do? . . . *WHAT?*' Otto clutched his head and rocked from side to side like a man who had reached the end of his tether . . .

It was the sight of the fat sergeant, squatting at the flank of the big black and white Holstein, gently milking the suddenly contented beast into his helmet with a practised finger, making soft reassuring sounds as he did so, that gave Otto his idea. New determination surged through his body and he felt the adrenalin pumping fresh energy into his bloodstream. Urgently he rose to his feet, towering above the men slumped in the wet grass all around him, waiting for new orders, 'Hey, you hayseed!' he called.

The fat sergeant looked up, a happy smile on his moonlike face. 'Yessir?' he called back.

'You're a farmer,' Otto cried. 'Do you think you can round up this little lot?'

'Why yes, sir, of course, sir,' the fat sergeant answered promptly, tapping the cow's flank, as if to reassure her he would be back, and rose to his feet, holding the helmet full of milk in his hand awkwardly. 'But what for, sir?'

Otto didn't answer directly. He frowned and said, 'Get rid of that cow-juice first – at the double.'

Reluctantly, the sergeant poured the milk out onto the grass and Otto snapped, 'I want you to drive the things towards the minefield.'

The sergeant gasped. 'You can't have me do that, sir!' he cried. 'Why the poor beasts might step on a mine and –'

'Exactly, you silly fart!' Otto cut in brutally. 'That is the shitting idea! Or would you like to go first and lead them personally?'

'No sir,' the sergeant answered and gulped, sudden tears in his eyes. 'But the beasts, the poor beasts.'

'Fuck the beasts! I've eaten bits o' em all my life, and so have you, comrade,' Otto said grimly, his hand falling significantly to his pistol holster. 'So don't be so shitting soft-hearted. *Nun wirds bald?*'

Reluctantly, very reluctantly, the ex-farmer picked up a branch and began to collect the doomed animals together.

The sergeant sobbed quietly, as the big heifer flew through the air and landed only metres away from him in a bundle of flailing, blood-red legs, lowing miserably. Now the field ahead of them was strewn with hideously wounded or dead cows, the smoke from the exploded mines drifting slowly over the awkward, heaving bodies, but failing to hide them from sight. All around Otto, the waiting infantrymen, bowed under their logs, stared open-mouthed and pale-faced at the massacred animals. Someone whispered, 'Shitting SS . . . cruel bastards . . . have no mercy.'

The words broke the heavy spell. Otto spun round, face flushed with rage. 'If I find the man who said that, I'll sew his arse up with twine – *so that he shits* through *his ears for the rest of his born days*!' Otto Stahl hated himself desperately at that particular moment; yet he knew there had been no other way to clear the minefield. Rather dumb animals than human beings, he told himself, though he wondered sometimes whether or not dumb animals were preferable to some of the human beings he knew. 'All right now, no more blabbering. Follow me.' Picking up his own log, he started to move forward cautiously, following the trail blazed by the unfortunate animals, the sergeant still sobbing softly behind him.

Five minutes later another blazing tram had just hurtled past them, its side bearing some impossible physical advice to the Führer, and they were ready to set to work. Now time was of the essence and Otto worked his soldiers all out, as they thrust home their logs, hastily forming a rough barrier just beneath the brow of the hill, reinforcing it with the heavy stones that lay everywhere. Sweating hard, the backs of their grey tunics black with perspiration, the infantrymen steadily raised the barrier, while to their front the Count lay in the grass, observing the American-held depot below and relaying a whispered commentary on the progress the GIs were making in their preparation of the next flame-monster.

'Three of them on the track . . .' he called. 'The driver's mounting the leading one . . . Half a dozen of their soldiers are giving it a shove-off . . . Won't be long now, Otto.'

'Los . . . los, Maenner!' Otto cried desperately. 'Move those slack arses! *Dalli . . . dalli . . .*' He aimed a hearty kick at the buttocks of the fat sergeant who was still sobbing miserably. *'MOVE IT!'*

'HERE IT COMES, OTTO!' the Count shrieked and rolled over away from the track hastily.

'OUT OF THE WAY!' Otto commanded desperately.

The infantrymen needed no urging. Hurriedly they flung themselves to left and right, scrambling frantically for cover, burying themselves deep into the steaming holes left by the exploded mines, bodies tensed, faces ashen with fear, as the roar grew ever closer and closer.

Crouched next to the Count, Otto felt his breath coming in short, hectic, almost painful gasps. His heart thumped madly, his nerves tingled with electric excitement. Would it work? Would the barrier hold and send the damn thing back the way it had come? If it didn't, would it explode here? Then they would all be finished and he had sacrificed the whole bunch of the stupid, hairy-assed stubble-hoppers needlessly.

The clatter and rattle was almost overwhelming now. He pushed the Count's head closer to the ground. 'Hold on to your hat, Count,' he yelled above the mad metallic racket. *'Here she comes!'*

The tram reared over the rise. It seemed to fill the whole world. Nothing could stop it. Otto watched in open-mouthed horror. His plan was not going to work, he knew it in his bones. Now the tram's speed started to increase once more. Angry blue sparks flew from its racing wheels. The thick black smoke from the tar barrels streamed behind it in the sudden tail-wind. Otto tensed, digging his nails into the palms of his sweat-lathered hands painfully. *NOW!*

The tram struck the barrier a tremendous blow. Wood splintered. Violet lights seared the length of the track. The tram wobbled and trembled alarmingly. It was going to come off the track. They were finished. Instinctively, Otto closed his eyes.

Suddenly it happened. The tram began to move backwards. Otto opened his eyes and stared as if seeing a ghost. But it was real. They had done it. The barrier had held.

'THE BUGGER'S GOING BACK, COUNT. BACK, DO YOU HEAR!' Otto threw all caution to the wind. He rose and raced after the tram as it laboured back up the incline the way it had come. He swung over the summit a moment after the tram. It hurtled towards the depot below at a tremendous rate. There, all was panic, confusion, chaos. Officers bellowed orders. NCOs shrilled, red-faced, on their whistles. A group of the GIs vainly tried to move the tram waiting there, already laden with barrels of tar and ammunition. But they quickly realized their danger. Moments later they were throwing themselves out of the vehicle and fleeing to all sides, as the other tram charged towards the stationary one.

Crump! The crash of the first explosion, accompanied by a blinding white flash, almost knocked Otto off his feet. He shook his head and held on desperately as the earth quivered and vibrated like a live thing beneath his feet. There was another tremendous thunderclap of sound. Amid an awesome rending of metal and splintering of wood, mingled with the snap-and-crackle of exploding small arms ammunition, the second tram rose high into the air to slap down again a moment later. For one long second nothing else happened. And then, with a great echoing roar that seemed to go on for ever and ever, the whole depot came tumbling down, as the GIs fled screaming for their lives, burying the other trams under tons of falling debris.

Otto sat down suddenly, all energy drained from him, as if someone had opened a tap. He had done it, and not a single life had been lost. There would be no more trams hurtling towards General von Schlackheimer's lines; now the leathery-faced old fart could return to fighting and killing the enemy in the usual conventional manner.

SEVEN

'*Splendid!*' the ancient general said with difficulty, as he lay flat on his stomach on the kitchen table, his breeches around his skinny shanks, while the mechanic repaired the defective joint of his artificial leg with a screwdriver. 'Absolutely splendid! I knew that I could rely on you stout fellahs of the SS.' He snorted with irritation, as the embarrassed corporal-mechanic fiddled with the knee joint, trying to keep his eyes off the general's ancient, flaccid organ which had dropped out of his underpants. 'Get on with it, man. I haven't got all day. Damn thing! Typical modern rubbish. Give me a good old reliable pegleg any day.' He forgot his irritation and said, 'But please, tell me more, Count.'

The Count looked at Otto, but the latter shrugged in a bored manner and looked out of the window. All Otto was interested in was the passes the general's adjutant was preparing for them at this very moment.

Outside the men of his late company, most of them heavily laden with bits and pieces they had sawn off the dead cows, were trying to find places where they could cook the fresh meat, followed by the envious gazes of the headquarters' staff. Even the fat sergeant who had cried, was busily washing a large chunk of raw meat. Otto grinned cynically and whispered to himself, '*Erst kommt das Fressen, dann die Moral*'[1] and turned back to watch the skinny old general spreadeagled on the kitchen table.

The perspiring soldier with the screwdriver was apparently finding his task a little difficult. His muscles bulged through his thin shirt, as he exerted all his strength to turn the screw in the knee joint. In a minute he'll have the old fart right off the table and onto the floor, Otto told himself,

[1] 'First grub, then morality.'

as the soldier virtually lifted the general up. But that wasn't to be. The screw turned and the soldier stepped back, clicked to attention and reported at the top of his voice, 'Screw in place, *sir*. Knee ready for duty, *sir*!'

The general grunted something and reached for his breeches. A moment later he was dressed again and on his feet, smiling fondly at Otto and the Count. 'Well, my two heroes,' he said. 'I suppose you will be off soon to the flesh-pots. My adjutant is preparing you a detailed map of how to get to – er – the place, where the fillies are. Damned fine gals! I can confidently say they have – er – done wonders for my outside plumbing ever since I got to know them.' He laughed creakily and made a surprisingly explicit obscene gesture with his fingers and thumb.

The Count flushed, and Otto told himself that with that ancient wrinkled piece of meat the dirty old shit had hanging between his legs, he'd need more than a wonder – he'd need a shitting first-class miracle!

'Herr General!'

They turned. It was the adjutant, elegant and efficient as befitted an adjutant. In his right hand, he held a briefcase. Otto's heart leaped at the sight. It would contain the promised leave-papers and the travel order. Now they would not have to rely on the American forgeries. These were the real things, signed by a genuine divisional commander. They certainly would see them through all the checkpoints to the rear of the front.

The adjutant marched forward and placed the briefcase on the table in front of the beaming general. *'Der Marschbefehl fur die Herren, Herr General,'* he barked.

'Thank you, Heinz.' The general took hold of the case and said, 'Well, gentlemen, I shall be sorry to lose two stout young officers like yourselves. But a promise is a promise, and you did get rid of those damned trams for me. As soon as I can get round to it, I'm going to have my personal thunderbox re-erected, now that it's safe again. Make a note of that, Heinz,' he added, shooting a quick look at the adjutant, 'divisional commander's latrine.'

'Yessir,' the adjutant replied promptly, whipping out his notebook and writing a few lines.

'And better put a guard on it. I won't have those common soldiers slipping in there behind my back to deposit their ordinary waste in my thunderbox.'

'Sir,' the adjutant answered, scribbling furiously.

'Better make it an officer guard – say – a second-lieutenant. I think my rank deserves that at least. A duty of such delicacy can, after all, only be entrusted to an officer. And make a little path of stones leading up to it, in case it rains.

'White-washed, sir?' the adjutant enquired, pausing.

'Excellent idea, Heinz. One likes a little bit of beauty around such a place. Good thinking.' The general beamed at the adjutant.

Otto looked up at the ceiling, as if praying to some God on high to give him strength. These generals were all alike, *all* the big-shots were. They seemed to believe in the Wagnerian myth that they were supermen without any ordinary human weaknesses. Did they really think that the ordinary hairy-assed stubble-hoppers thought their generals shat through their ribs or something?

'You could put a little ration can with a few nice flowers in there, too, Heinz,' the general suggested, carried away by the heady business of the new latrine. 'At my age, unfortunately, one takes longer – and it would be rather jolly to look at something pretty while one's waiting for nature to take its course, what!'

The adjutant frowned. 'Bit difficult, sir. The time of year, you know. They'd have to be paper.'

Now it was the general's turn to frown. 'Paper, eh,' he said thoughtfully. 'Aren't there any spring flowers about? We could send out a patrol into the woods to see if they could find some early primroses or . . .'

The sudden roar of racing airplane engines drowned the rest of his words, as all around the farmhouse headquarters the light flak opened up at the intruders. Otto flung a startled glance out of the window. Two bright silver birds were zooming in at tree-top height, cannon chattering, white tracer shells racing for the house in lethal fury. '*Jabos . . . enemy Jabos!*'[1] he yelled.

In that very same instant a white-faced signals officer burst into the room unceremoniously, waving a message form and crying in sudden panic, 'Montgomery's attacked, sir! The enemy's crossing the Rhine in full strength, sir. It's the big attac . . ttack . . .' Abruptly he was slurring his words in a strange, inexplicable manner, his legs beginning to give way beneath him like those of a new-born foal, what looked like steam rising from between his hunched shoulders.

The Count made as if he were going to rush to help the dying officer, as the general forgot his latrine and cried, '*Sound the alarm! . . . They're coming . . . Sound the alarm, Heinz!*'

In the same instant that the signals officer slapped to the floor dramatically, a great hole ripped in the small of his back by the burst of shells which had penetrated the roof, Otto grabbed the precious briefcase, propelled the Count in front of him towards the door, and cried over his shoulder at the excited old general, 'Going to alert the men, sir . . . *Auf wiedersehn*!'

Five minutes later, watched by their company, still holding the uncooked meat a little helplessly like a bunch of frustrated butchers waiting for customers, the two old friends disappeared into the woods for good . . .

'*That was the morning of 24 March, 1945*,' Otto told me the last time I saw him before he pulled off his historic coup and vanished for ever. 'I suppose I knew even then that it was an assault and a date that were heading straight for the history books. It was only later that I realized that it had gone into Otto's own personal account of World War Two. You'd better believe it, Leo. Because on that day, even as the Count and I were running for our shitting lives through those woods, before the general caught up with us and ordered us back to the firing-line, I knew Frau Stahl's

[1] Dive-bombers.

handsome son – God bless the old cow wherever she might be today – had survived yet again.

'Of course, I'm a good survivor. Any sensible person in my profession, Leo, has got to be. The question, then, was – *to what purpose*, had I survived?

'There were six weeks of the war to go yet, though, of course, I didn't know it at the time. But once the Tommies and the Amis crossed the Rhine in strength, I guessed it was curtains for the Reich. Old Adolf had finally had it. But what was in it for me, I asked myself. What was I gonna loot from the wreck, eh, Leo?

'I'd been purple-shafted as a spy for old Hitler, nearly buggered by Churchill's by-blow, raped by the Russian female commissar, conned over and over again by Patton and Montgomery, nearly sent to Leavenworth prison for life by the feller who was supposed to be Eisenhower – and what had I got out of it. *Nix!*

'That March afternoon, Leo, as the Count and I finally crawled into a nice cosy little hideout in the woods to think out what to do next, Frau Stahl's handsome son told himself he was going to get his revenge on the whole bloody system – and make some dough out of it at the same time! Yessir, Leo! There was some money to be made out of the end of the Third Reich somewhere or other and I was going to be the one that made it . . . The only thing I didn't know that afternoon, with the shitting guns roaring and the rain belting down, as if God and his angels themselves were pissing on us, was that it was going to take forty frigging years to make it . . .'

I suppose that last conversation with Otto Stahl should have warned me that he had something up his sleeve. But as we sat on the terrace of that modest little villa he owned, staring out at the green, mirror-like surface of the Med, I was more concerned to record Otto's account of the last year of the war. I should have noticed that the living room was packed with the biographies of the National Socialist leaders. The Fests, the Masers, the Tolands were all well represented – and they had obviously been well read. There were those embarrassing pictures from *Stern* magazine stuck up on the walls as well. A bespectacled, slightly dishevelled, Lord Dacre testifying that the Hitler Diaries were absolutely genuine at that celebrated press conference in Hamburg. The reporter who had discovered them posing proudly in front of the old yacht which had once belonged to 'Fat Herman' himself, *Reichsmarschall* Goering. The blow-up of the famous forgeries themselves with those elaborate gold initials 'AH' for Adolf Hitler.

It was all there to warn me. When had Otto ever read a book, except for those neutral-covered ones that he had smuggled into Spain and had been forced to resort to 'because the frigging old salami won't get stiff any frigging more,' as he would explain angrily (and that when he was servicing a dark-eyed beauty from Andalucia, who couldn't have been a day over eighteen!)? What interest had Otto ever shown in the lives of the Nazi 'Greats'? '*A load of brown-uniformed farts*,' he was wont to describe his former leaders with a snort of indignation. '*Megalomania-mongers, the whole rotten bunch of them . . . On the make . . . out for frigging grabs!*'

As for the *Stern* magazine, he had harboured only contempt for West Germany's leading illustrated. Once, when I had suggested we approach Herr Nenri Nannen[1] and attempt to sell his, Otto's, memoirs to the Hamburg publication, he had snarled, 'It won't go, Leo. Don't even bother. They won't buy my story. All them friggers on the *Rotenbaumchaussee*[2] can think of is getting a new pair of female tits on the front cover so that they can sell the frigging thing! They can stick the *Stern*, Leo!'

I should have known then, shouldn't I? All the signs were there. The very look on Otto's wrinkled, but cunning, old face should have told me that summer. He was up to his old tricks again. I didn't tumble to what Otto was up to, alas. But then, in general, authors are unworldly, naive people, aren't they just . . . and Otto Stahl is . . . well Otto Stahl!

1 Publisher of the *Stern* magazine.
2 The home of the magazine in Central Hamburg.

BOOK TWO: THE CAPTAINS DEPART

'Besser ein Ende mit Schrecken als ein Schrecken ohne Ende'.

Popular German saying of spring 1945[1]

[1]Roughly: 'Better an end with terror than a terror without an end.'

ONE

As the thin wail of the air-raid sirens sounded the 'all-clear' over Lübeck and the thunder of the flak began to die away, they took up their conversation once more in that villa on the edge of the port which now housed the Swedish consulate.

The pasty-faced SS general with the schoolmaster's pince-nez firmly attached to his nose persisted in his attitude. 'I have sworn loyalty to Adolf Hitler and as a soldier and as a German, Count Bernadotte,' he said, 'I cannot go back on my oath. Because of this I cannot do anything in opposition to the Führer's plans and wishes.'

Behind the general's back, the sleek-haired young SD officer, who had arranged this meeting between his chief and the representative of the Swedish Government, Count Bernadotte, frowned. Bernadotte frowned, too. He knew that secret service officer Schellenberg had only one object in mind now – to leave the sinking ship before it was too late. Schellenberg had the utmost interest in attempting to convince his chief to negotiate with the Western Allies, with or without Hitler's approval. But his chief remained obstinately unwilling to make that move.

For a moment or two there was silence, broken only by the muted siren of an ambulance outside, heading for the centre of the burning city. Bernadotte studied the face of the most feared man in Europe once again, searching for a clue to his character. It was a puffy, rather commonplace face. The chin was weak and receding too, the hands matched it; they were small, well-manicured, almost feminine. Only the eyes behind that schoolmaster's pince-nez, blue-grey and hard, seemed to show strength of will. Otherwise Heinrich Himmler, the head of the SS and the Third Reich's feared notorious police *apparat*, could have well been some third-grade clerk in one of his own provincial police offices.

Schellenberg, the oily ex-lawyer who knew that Germany was finished and that anything he might do to please the Allies could well save him from the hangman's rope – for that was where they were all heading, if nothing was done about it soon – broke the heavy brooding silence. '*Reichsführer*,' he said desperately, 'the Führer is a sick, very sick, man. Totally paralysed and suffering from Parkinson's disease. In all frankness, sir, he is no longer in control. Someone like you must take over the reins, make decisions, attempt to win something out of the defeat for our poor suffering people – before it is too late.'

Passionately, while Bernadotte smoked and nodded his approval, the SD officer worked on his chief, trying to break down the idolized Hitler in Himmler's eyes, to convince the latter that he was the second Führer, the second incarnation of the spirit of that Aryan Germany, all gigantic blond youths and laughing, big-bosomed blue-eyed maidens, about which the little man with the pince-nez was always enthusing. 'You must take charge, sir. Make the decisions which just *have* to be made,' Schellenberg said urgently. 'Someone has to talk to the representatives of the Western Allies and only you, *Reichsführer*, are big enough and bold enough to take that step. *Not* Goering! *Not* Goebbels! *Not* Bormann! No sir,' Schellenberg raised one finger and wagged it furiously, as if he were still addressing the court in the days when he had still been a provincial lawyer. 'Only you, *Heinrich Himmler!*' He gasped and stared at his chief, as if he were seeing him for the very first time. Bernadotte waited expectantly.

'So you are demanding I depose the Führer?' Himmler asked slowly. 'There is no other way, you know.'

Bernadotte tensed. Schellenberg could well hang for this.

Schellenberg rose to the bait. He sprang to his feet, fake tears in his dark, cunning eyes. 'As much as it hurts me to say this, sir,' he declared dramatically, 'I must tell you the truth. The answer is yes. You *must* depose the Führer!'

Himmler swallowed hard, his prominent Adam's apple whipping up and down his neck, as if carried back and forth by an express lift. 'Do you really think so, Schellenberg?'

'I *know* so, sir. Our only chance to save what is left of our beloved Fatherland is to empower Count Bernadotte here to go to Eisenhower with a personal offer of discussions with him to arrange a ceasefire in the West. You, sir, can deal with the East in due course. Eisenhower will very probably turn the German Army loose on the Russians and ensure that they are wiped out for good. The Americans are a tidy people. They like things cleaned up once and for all, it's the only way to do business.'

Himmler brightened up. 'Do you really think so, Schellenberg?' he asked eagerly.

'Yessir. All our information is,' Schellenberg lied glibly, 'that the Anglo-Americans are prepared to march against the Reds once they have terminated the war against ourselves. If you acted now, sir, you could well get in on the – er – ground floor, as the Americans say.'

Himmler pursed his thin lips thoughtfully. 'Give me five minutes with General Eisenhower,' he said slowly, 'and I am sure I could convince him. Get him out of those Jewish advisers who surround him and I am certain we could come to some sort of arrangement.'

Outside in the hall the grandfather clock slowly and sombrely struck midnight. Himmler rose to his feet, reminded that he had a lot to do this night before it grew light and the Allied *jabos* filled the skies over North Germany once more, making all movement highly dangerous. Reluctantly Schellenberg rose, too.

'We shall see, *Herr Graf*,' Himmler announced, reaching for his cap with the dreaded silver skull-and-crossbones of the SS. 'I have some further urgent appointments this night. Very hush-hush, you know.' He touched the side of his nose with the German gesture, importantly. 'Matters of state. But I shall be contacting you again very soon . . .' Suddenly he seemed embarrassed, '. . . about the thing we have just discussed.'

'Yes, *Reichsführer*,' Bernadotte protested. 'But time is of the essence. The Anglo-Americans have already crossed the Rhine. It won't be long now before . . .'

But the most feared man in Europe was no longer listening.

Five minutes later he and Schellenberg had disappeared into the night in their sleek black Mercedes, leaving Count Bernadotte to shake his head and declare to the inquiring First Secretary, 'Nothing, Sven, absolutely nothing! His people are dying by the thousand every day that dawns. The Allies are over the Rhine, the Russians are approaching Berlin and tomorrow the Allied air forces will continue their destruction of what is left of Germany's cities, and *still* he can't make up his mind to get rid of that madman in Berlin and make peace.' He shook his head in mock wonder. 'Germans – crazy as loons, the lot of 'em! Always were . . . *always will be* . . .'

She was waiting for him as he unlocked the door of the discreet villa he had rented for her just outside Lübeck. She had rested already, for the left side of her pretty face was wrinkled from the pillow, but loyal little darling that she was, his favourite peppermint tea was still warming on the little stove and there was a plate of sweet biscuits on the table.

'Heini, my little Harrykins,' she cried and swept towards him, dressing-gown flying open to reveal the nakedness beneath. 'Your slippers are warming inside the stove. I put another briquet on before I lay down . . .'

Gently, he held her away from him and said, 'I am sorry, little mother, I am afraid there will be no time for such indulgence this night – and perhaps for a long time to come, *schnuggi*.'

His youthful mistress's face fell and her bottom lip trembled, as if she might break down and weep at any moment.

Hurriedly he pressed her hand. A German maiden should never cry; she should be hard as Krupp steel, everyone knew that. 'Do not cry, my little cheetah,' he urged, pressing hard. 'There are affairs of state to be attended to. Great things –' He stopped short. In her agitation, she had released her gown once more and it had fallen open to reveal all her opulent charms. 'My girl,' he breathed hard, his glasses suddenly steaming over, 'you'll catch your death of cold without your – er,' he coughed delicately, raising his hand to his mouth as etiquette demanded, 'underthings on.'

'But it is so long, Harrykins, since you last favoured me,' she pouted, suddenly petulant. 'And I was so looking forward to a wee hour with you this night . . . I even allowed myself the luxury of a bath,' she added a little guiltily, for she knew that her lover was very keen that his 'folk-comrades' should not waste water, 'instead of waiting till Saturday night.'

Himmler did not seem to hear. His eyes were fixed on her delightful body, plump and white, adorned by the hairy black triangle at its base, suddenly full of sexual interest. 'It's these damned boots, you know,' he whispered hoarsely, eyes focusing on her firm breasts, 'so hard to get them off and on in a hurry – and I'm afraid I am in a hurry this night, little mother.'

'No matter, Harrykins,' she said with sudden excitement, her eyelashes fluttering wildly, her nipples abruptly standing out like red bottle-tops. 'No need for you to take off your things.' Her hand reached out greedily for the sudden bulge in his breeches. 'We could simply lower our breeches. It would be *romantisch*, like in the old days in the office.' She gave a kind of horselike whinny, as her hand closed on his organ, and sagged back against the table as if she might faint at any moment.

'Do you really think we could!' he gasped hoarsely, already fumbling with his issue braces, decorated delicately by Gertrud herself with swastikas stitched in pink silk.

'Of course, of course,' she cried. 'Quick . . . Harrykins!' Still holding on to him, she stumbled backwards to the couch, dragging him with her as he ripped at his breeches with fingers that felt like clumsy sausages . . .

*

It was thus that *Obergruppenführer* Walter Schellenberg, who had received no answer to his persistent knocking (though he should have been alerted by the regular, hectic squeaking of the couch springs from within), found his master and his secretary, as he opened the door. *Reichsführer* SS Heinrich Himmler, with his leather coat flung about his shoulders and his breeches round his ankles, to reveal his skinny yellow buttocks, as he humped a great mountain of a woman, all dangling dugs and massive thighs, like some undersized alpinist trying to ascend Everest.

'*Reichsführer!*' he exclaimed in surprise.

Himmler started and paused in mid-stroke.

Gertrud closed her eyes and pretended that Schellenberg wasn't there. 'More, Harrykins, you naughty boy. Give me more, or little mother will be angry with Harrykins . . . Have to spank Harrykins,' she whispered huskily, making little groaning, moaning sounds, tortured as she was by some private ecstasy. 'No, please, Harrykins . . . Don't take it away . . . *Harrykins*!'

But it was already too late. That little tube of delightful flesh was fast shrinking, sliding away remorselessly, back from the dripping slippery cavern, gone for good, never to be recalled, already history. Never again would it slam so delightfully against the tickler, rub against the serrated flesh, plunge into the furthest reaches of that dripping chamber to discharge its white fury so beautifully. The man who had once held three hundred million Europeans from the Channel to the Urals in his sway, Heinrich Himmler, had failed to achieve his last orgasm.

'Just testing Fraulein Gertrud's pulse, Schellenberg,' he breathed, fumbling to do up his flies. 'She came over a little faint suddenly.'

'Yessir,' Schellenberg answered dutifully, not daring to look at Gertrud who sprawled on the couch still, plump white legs raised in the air expectantly, eyes screwed tightly closed.

'Yes, in these parlous times, even our young people are overcome easily,' Himmler said, ripping up his braces to reveal the legend that his mistress had embroidered so lovingly beneath the pink swastikas. '*HOME IS WHERE A WARRIOR HANGS HIS HELMET, XMAS 1943.*'

'Yessir,' Schellenberg answered dutifully.

'I wonder if you would go into the hall for a few moments. I have a few last minute instructions I would like to give to Fraulein Geilhorn.'

'Naturally, sir. Of course, sir.' Schellenberg went out, keeping his gaze discreetly lowered.

Immediately Gertrud opened her eyes and grabbed for Himmler's loins once more.

He backed away hastily. 'No, little mother. No more time for the pleasures of the flesh now, I'm afraid. Duty must always come first.'

'But, Harrykins –'

He held up his hand for silence. 'No. Now listen to me. You must leave this place for good as soon as it is dark tomorrow night. I have made all the arrangements. There will be an armoured car and bodyguard commanded by an officer for you. All good loyal fellows from the SS, tried and tested at the front.'

'But where am I going, Harrykins?' she asked, reluctantly doing up her robe and hiding those breasts from him for the last time, though, of course, he did not know it then.

'A long, long way from here, little mother,' he said, daring to pat her hand. 'To another country,' he added mysteriously.

Her plump, silly face fell again, as if she might cry. 'When will I ever see you again, Harrykins, when? A foreign country. It is too much for a poor weak woman to bear.'

'Never fear,' he said with false heartiness, reaching for his cap. 'We will meet again – soon. But you must be brave like our German women of old were brave.'

Outside there was the sound of a car engine being revved up impatiently. 'I must go, little mother.'

'*Heinrich!*'

'*Gertrud!*'

They flung themselves into each other's arms in a passionate embrace, faces noble yet contorted with grief, like stage lovers in some third-rate melodrama. The driver sounded his horn as if impatient to be off; for everyone in Himmler's escort knew that they had to reach Schloss Wewelsberg before dawn, if they didn't want to be attacked by the Allied air gangsters.

Himmler released himself hurriedly. 'Little mother, I must go.' He placed his cap firmly on his cropped head.

She burst into tears. 'Heinrich,' she wailed. '*NO!*'

But already he was sailing through the door towards the waiting Mercedes.

A moment later she heard it draw away down the street, gaining speed by the instant. Heart-broken she collapsed sobbing into the couch, which sagged alarmingly under her considerable weight.

'When . . . when will I see him again, *mein Führer*?' she gulped, addressing the picture of Adolf Hitler adorning the opposite wall.

Hitler did not answer.

For a while Fraulein Gertrud Geilhorn, known behind her back by obviously envious colleagues, who had not enjoyed the *Reichsführer* SS's favours, as 'Miss Randy Horn'[1] continued to sob, her plump shoulders heaving, as if her heart were broken. Then she remembered she had not eaten anything since *Abendbrot* and it was well past midnight. Idly at first, then quite greedily, she started to nibble at the biscuits that she had put out for dear Harrykins. As an afterthought she poured herself a cup of peppermint tea to wash them down with. After a while she decided she could stand a kirsch, too. By two o'clock that April morning, as Himmler sped through the night to meet his black knights at far-off Wewelsberg, 'Miss Randy Horn' was sprawled on her back on the couch, snoring heartily, drunk and dead to the world . . .

[1] *Geil* means 'randy' in German.

TWO

The Thunderbolt fell startlingly out of a perfect morning sky. A flash of silver, a murderous howl of its big radial engine, and it was zooming in at 400mph, cannon already chattering frenetically.

'*Jabo . . . Ami Jabo!*' the frightened cry went up on all sides down the length of the long column of weary soldiers and civilians. Immediately they panicked. Screaming with fear, they broke to left and right, fighting and clawing each other in their terror-stricken haste, fleeing to the safety of the fields.

Another enemy plane roared in. Tracer bullets ripped the length of the road. An old nag sagged between the traces, blood jetting out of multiple wounds in scarlet arcs. Cannon pumped white death at the fleeing civilians. A child went down, hands fanning the air, back ripped open and steaming hotly where the shells had penetrated. A cart went up in flames – and then yet another. Suddenly all was terror, noise, cruel death.

Otto flung the startled Count into a ditch and pressed his head into the mud and nettles at the bottom. 'Get down . . . For Christsake, get down, Count! Here come more of the murderous bastards!' He ducked hurriedly as a Thunderbolt came racing in at tree-top height, machine-guns blazing, its engine howling, so big that it seemed to fill the whole world.

Shells exploded all around the terrified civilians cowering in the ditch. Otto felt the momentary searing heat as they ripped past his bent back, to explode in a flurry of soil in the field beyond. A woman screamed shrilly. Otto risked a look. A few metres away a woman suckling a child to her breast had been hit. Even before he could reach her, she reeled backwards, already dead, the infant wailing pitifully at her lifeless breast.

O. H. L. L.—4

Another wave of the dreaded dive-bombers came howling in, as Otto bent over the woman. They raced to the attack, as if this were a hugely enjoyable game, weaving from side to side, waggling their wings, some of them even lowering their undercarriages so that their planes were slowed down and they could aim better. All of them new, well-fed, confident men, who had never known defeat, knew the Krauts were beaten; that what few planes the *Luftwaffe* had left were fully occupied trying to protect Germany's cities; that these miserable refugees were theirs for the taking, to kill or leave alive just as they wished.

Suddenly Otto forgot his own danger. He was seized by a burning, unreasoning rage. He stumbled to his feet, eyes blazing, and tugged out his pistol. Like some latterday David facing up to a flying Goliath, he stood there, the bullets ploughing the earth all around him unheeded, firing at the silver planes, as they swept over the column, leaving death and destruction behind them, before soaring high into the bright blue sky, twisting and turning excitedly in their victory rolls.

'Bastards!' Otto roared impotently behind them, as the child cried at his feet and the refugees started to pop their heads cautiously above the edge of the ditch, 'murdering American bastards . . . killing innocent women and kids . . .!'

Gently, the Count put his arm round his shaking young friend and said, 'Don't take on, Otto, please . . . It's war, you must understand, war, my boy.'

Otto turned on him, eyes blazing with an almost unbearable rage, 'War you say! . . . No, never. This,' he extended a dirty hand at the dead civilians slumped like abandoned bundles of old rags on the road everywhere, 'is not war, Count! It's a massacre, pure and simple . . . a *bloody massacre*!' Suddenly Otto's shoulders slumped and he started to weep.

Gently the Count led him to the cover of some trees and sat him down, patting his heaving shoulders all the time.

*

The two old comrades had been on the road three days now; and it was clear even to the Count that the days of the Third Reich were numbered. With the exception, perhaps, of the young fanatics of the armed SS, who still held their positions to the 'last man and the last bullet', as the High Command in Berlin demanded, the rest of the *Wehrmacht* was in full retreat. Everywhere, the roads were packed with long weary columns of the field-greys, many of them without weapons, their officers already gone. Behind them they left their tanks and armoured vehicles, not even bothering to immobilize them, leaving them for the pursuing armoured columns to capture intact.

For their part the Americans advanced confidently and brutally. Now all the American tankers subscribed to Patton's 'German War Memorial' theory. Every village in the path of the tanks, whether it was defended or not, was subjected to heavy artillery fire first, before it was stormed by the armoured infantry. Thus every inhabited place would be left with its 'war memorial', a score of shattered houses, a permanent reminder that the Americans had once passed this way in the Big War. The American Air Force was just as brutal. Unopposed now by the *Luftwaffe*, they ranged far and wide, totally free agents, shooting up everything and anything that moved during the daylight hours.

Time and time again in these last three terrible days, Otto and the Count had come across little country roads, packed with dead women, children and old men, caught out in the open as they fled northwards before the American armour, slaughtered mercilessly by those unthinking young men from the New World.

Once they had been startled while resting, footsore and weary at the side of a track, by the slow, tired clip-clop of a horse. They had turned to see an ancient, sway-backed mare coming towards them, pulling a battered farmcart behind it, packed high with pathetic little bits and pieces of furniture, on which people appeared to be slumped, sleeping. There had been no driver on the seat. But the old mare seemed to know the way without benefit of driver.

When the cart had finally come level with them, they

had seen to their horror that the civilians were not sleeping. They were dead! They had been shot from the air, as they crouched there. Their bodies were frozen thus, as if for all time. Horrified, rooted to the ground, they had watched as that cart of death creaked by, the old mare towing its cargo of horror, as if it would carry on thus for ever . . .

Now the two comrades had yet again witnessed a massacre of harmless civilians and Otto had had enough. As the survivors resumed their weary progress northwards, a slow collection of farmcarts, bicycles, prams, even a few hand-barrows and carts towed by ropes, Otto raised his head and said, 'Count, I've had enough of this. Let us find this shitting Wewelsberg Castle, signal the Amis to bomb hell out of it, and then forget the bastards once and for all.'

'I agree for once,' Count von der Weide said solemnly. 'I am afraid that the Americans are making us pay a too heavy price for having lost the war.' He indicated a group of drunken stubble-hoppers who had flung away their weapons, even their helmets, and who were now reeling from side to side of the body-littered road, bawling out some marching-song or other. 'They will never fight again – nor will the mass of the German army for that matter. Why, then, persecute us any more? Germany is finished.'

'That it is, Count,' Otto said, new determination in his voice as he wiped the tears from his eyes a little shamefacedly. 'And we'll be finished with it, if we're not careful.' He rose to his feet, fists clenched, jaw hard and set. 'But I don't see why we should go out of it empty-handed. In three devils' name, we've withstood the horror of this war as much as any hairy-assed front swine! Why shouldn't we get something out of it before it is too late?'

'But what, Otto?' the Count asked a little helplessly, as he rose, too, trying to keep his eyes off the dead.

'Everyone knows that the Golden Pheasants[1] have been lining their pockets ever since 1933. Do you think that

[1] Contemptuous nickname for Nazi Party officials on account of their liking for gold braid.

Himmler is any different?' Count von der Weide opened his mouth, but Otto beat him to it. 'Of course not!' he sneered contemptuously. 'That four-eyed, knock-kneed shit has been stacking it away, year in, year out, just like the rest of those brown bastards. The question is,' Otto's eyes grew cunning, 'where has he hidden the loot?'

It was a rhetorical question and the Count knew it. 'You mean Wewelsberg Castle, Otto?'

'Where else?' Otto replied. 'That place has been the centre of the SS's mumbo-jumbo – all that Aryan blond, Wagner crap – since old Adolf came to power. It stands to reason that Himmler has got his loot salted away there. Why else do you think he's due there soon? Now, when the whole bloody thing is falling to pieces? Not to rattle the bones and give the other SS big-shots the secret handshake and all that kind of crap.' Otto's face contorted in angry contempt. 'No, not on yer shitting life, Count! Himmler is heading for Wewelsberg to pick up the dibs so that he can make dust before it is too shitting late.'

'Do you really think so, Otto?' the Count breathed, eyes full of admiration for his young friend's acumen.

'I *know* so,' Otto said confidently. 'Himmler's not going to hang about and wait for the Amis to string him up to the nearest lamp-post. No sir! That shit has got his head screwed on the right way. He's gonna do a bunk. But *not* if Frau Stahl's handsome son, Otto, has any say in it.'

'But what can we do about it, Otto?' the Count protested. 'Just the two of us against the whole of the SS?'

Otto winked one eye slowly and solemnly. He tapped the bulge in his tunic. 'Have you forgotten the old J-E transmitter, Count?' he asked.

'You mean that apparatus that Colonel Ersenbrick gave you before we set out?'

'Exactly.' Once again, Otto tapped the top-secret device which was securely strapped to his ribs. 'Just the two of us, you said, Count. Oh ye of little faith.' He clasped his hands together in mock piety, eyes raised to heaven. 'What was it that sanctimonious old fart Ersenbrick said to us back there? To him that believeth, all things are possible. *A-shitting-men!*'

The Count looked worried. 'One shouldn't blaspheme, Otto, not at a time like this.' He looked at the sky, as if he half-expected a divine thunderbolt to come hurtling down to strike Otto dead on the spot.

But his young friend laughed easily. 'Hell, Count, don't worry about God. He's forgotten the Germans this year.' His face grew serious. 'Count, it is *not* just the two of us. With the help of the little old J-E here, we've got the whole frigging US Army Air Corps at our disposal. Just for the calling . . . Now listen, this is what we're gonna do . . .'

THREE

'*Schloss Wewelsberg*,' Otto announced, as the two of them crouched there in the silver darkness, staring up at the Gothic pile, outlined a stark hard black against the star-studded night sky, dominating the plain below as it had done these thousand years or more ever since the early Saxon princes had built it.

Now, however, it was not defended by archers and the odd giant catapult-throwing rocks, but by multiple flak batteries, dug in everywhere around the castle, the long barrels of their 88mm cannon clearly visible to the two lone observers. In addition, they noted the field guns and the squat shapes of Mark III tanks stationed at the base of the hill.

'They say, Otto,' the Count said in a small voice, a little awed by that vast expanse of sky and the great castle above, 'that Himmler indulges in strange rites up there. He never allows more than twelve guests, all picked from the highest echelons of the SS, to be present at his table, like King Arthur and the Knights of the Round Table . . . and that down in the crypt, they already have their own graves dug, complete with coat-of-arms . . . They call it . . . the Realm of the Dead.' He shivered a little. 'They say that he believes in a local legend that, just as in the days when the Saxons were fighting the Slavs on this very same plain a thousand years ago, there will be only one survivor of the next assault from the east – and that will be the Lord of Wewelsberg Castle . . . It's all very strange, and a bit eerie, Otto, don't you think?'

'Oh, for crying out loud, knock it off, Count, or yer'll have me pissing in my boots!'

'Please, must you be so crude, Otto,' the Count said sulkily.

Otto did not seem to notice. Instead he concentrated his

gaze on the castle. It was a typical early medieval structure, rebuilt, he guessed, in the seventeenth century in a massive triangular form. It was just the place, he told himself, to capture the diseased imagination of a crank like Himmler, with his head full of all that Wagnerian, Aryan bullshit. Still it would be a formidable nut to crack. 'It looks a tough place to get into, Count,' he mused, breaking his own silence. He tweaked the end of his nose. 'Those walls 'd be damn hard to scale.'

'Why don't we go in through the front gate then?' the Count said simply.

'And what's that supposed to shitting well mean?'

'This, my boy. We have the uniform and the papers. I am sure those guards down there at the base of the place will be SS, too. Why should they stop us?'

'But our papers state we are on our way to Berlin to have a little gallop with two fillies, as that old fart of a general put it – well, on leave at least.'

'So.' The Count shrugged easily. 'The whole of Germany is in chaos. The transport system – roads and rails – is completely messed up. What should two brave SS officers, highly decorated to boot, do in such circumstances? Why forgo their leave and volunteer to fight to the last for their beloved *Reichsführer*.'

'Hey, not so much of that fight to the last thing,' Otto said darkly, as he considered the idea.

He knew that, if his plan was to work, he had to get inside the mysterious castle which was the heart of the black legend that Himmler had created for his SS. Before he could set the Americans up and flush the *Reichsführer* SS out, he first had to discover if the four-eyed shit was inside. In addition, he had to case the joint and work out the lay-out, the floor plan, because once the balloon went up, they'd have to be in and out with the loot at top speed.

'I think, Count, you have the right idea,' he conceded finally after some thought. 'When do you think we should have a crack at it?'

The Count shrugged easily. 'Why not strike while the iron's hot, Otto, my boy? Why not *now*?'

The guard at the side entrance, helmeted and very wide awake, in spite of the hour, examined their papers very thoroughly. Otto and the Count, their hearts thumping furiously, stood in the circle of blue light, trying to appear nonchalant and bored by the whole business, the Count yawning every now and again in a manner which seemed to a nervous, very tense Otto, to be fake and theatrical.

Surprisingly enough the sentry fell for it. 'I am very sorry, gentlemen, to keep you like this,' he said, handing them back the travel documents. 'I know you must be exhausted, the way the roads are just now. But I have the strictest orders from the duty officer. When the *Reichsführer* is in residence, he says we can't be too careful, gentlemen.'

Otto's heart leapt excitedly. So Himmler *was* at Wewelsberg after all! The sentry nodded to the other guard standing by the red-and-white pole which barred their way. 'You may pass, gentlemen,' he said and clicked to attention. 'You'll find the duty officer on the second floor, room L-52. He will provide you with sleeping accommodation.'

Casually, as befitted a much decorated SS front-swine, the Count touched his hand to his cap. 'Thank you, soldier. I shall ensure –'

He did not finish. Somewhere a bell had begun to toll sombrely. The young SS man grinned. 'Midnight mass, sir, that's what we call it down here. The generals are going to say their prayers down in the crypt.' Still smiling, as if at some private joke, he ushered them through before they could ask any further questions.

They moved hesitantly, through a small iron gate. A huge stone runic SS loomed up starkly against the silver night sky. They walked by, instinctively heading towards the tolling of the bell. They entered the castle. Now everywhere they could hear the creaking of the ancient wooden floors as unseen persons hurried to 'midnight mass', as the sentry had called it, and the candles flickered abruptly as doors were opened and the draught penetrated into the hall, throwing their shadows onto the wall. The Count shuddered suddenly.

'What is it?' Otto asked, feeling as apprehensive as the Count. There was something eerie about this place; he didn't like it one bit.

'A louse ran over my liver, Otto, that's all,' the Count answered.

'Mine, too,' Otto agreed. 'With bloody big hobnail boots on! Come on, let's see what's going on.'

They passed from the hall into a huge dining-room, dominated by a great oaken table that was at least thirty metres long, surrounded by high pig-skin chairs, each bearing a little silver plate. In the light of the waving candles, which threw their shadows in grotesque distortion on the walls, the Count bent and read a few of the names aloud. 'Berger . . . Wolff . . . Dietrich . . .'

'All the SS big shots,' Otto said, recognizing the last name from his abortive encounter with the Bavarian general during the Battle of the Bulge[1]. 'Holy strawsack and I bet they didn't dine off a bit of ration sausage on that shitting table. Half a cow each at least, I'll be bound!'

Now the tolling of the bell was growing ever louder and more insistent. The shuffling of many feet came closer, too, and from down the corridor that led off the huge dining-hall there was the flickering of torches. Suddenly the cold, stale air was fragrant with the scent of resin and burning pine.

'*Quick*, Count, duck, behind the table!' Otto urged. 'They're coming this way!'

Hurriedly, the two friends hid themselves behind the massive pig-skin chairs, nerves jingling with electric tension, hardly daring to breathe, as the procession shuffled into the room, the fiery reflection of their torches executing a wild, mad dance on the walls.

[1] See *Otto and the SS* for further details.

Cautiously, very cautiously, Otto peered out from behind his cover.

A long line of SS officers, all clad in their pre-war black uniforms, their chests ablaze with decorations, one hand clasped on their ivory-hilted ceremonial daggers, the other bearing a crackling pine resin torch, were shuffling forward, heads bent piously like monks preparing to mumble their nocturnal devotions in the chapel. But it wasn't the mass of SS officers, all of them giants, which made Otto gasp. It was the little group of men at the head of the procession. Each of them was obviously a very senior officer to judge by the swords they carried, and all were clad in a long black robe, bearing the SS rune on one shoulder and what looked like a coat-of-arms on the other.

'Shit on the shingle,' Otto whispered to the Count, as the procession shuffled by, 'do you think we've bumped into a meeting of the Tommies' House of Lords, Count?'

'Not exactly. But did you see who was leading those senior officers, Otto?'

'No. Who?'

'The man we're looking for,' the Count replied excitedly. 'No less than Heinrich Himmler himself!'

'Are you sure?' Otto hissed excitedly.

'Certain, absolutely certain of it. I met him several times before the war when I worked for Father Christmas[1]. In those days Himmler was quite interested in the Great Game and –'

'Oh shut up about the shitting Great Game!' Otto hissed and rose to his feet. 'Come on,' he commanded. 'Let's see what this little lot are up to at this time of night. Move it!'

Reluctantly, Count von der Weide 'moved it'.

They had followed the rest of that silent procession down flight after flight of stone stairs, the only sound the uncanny eerie stamp of the SS officers' boots on the worn stone, getting ever deeper until now they were in the crypt itself,

[1] Admiral Canaris, the head of the German Secret Service, nicknamed 'Father Christmas' on account of his snowy white hair.

buried in the very heart of the hill on which the castle had been built so many centuries before. Crowded in the back of the crypt, its dripping stone walls hung with huge black banners bearing the silver runic insignia of the SS Field Divisions, the skeleton key of the 'Bodyguard', the 'HJ' of the 'Hitler Youth', the mailed fist of the 'Goetz vom Berchlingen', the only light, that given off by giant silver oil lamps which sent their flames to the vented stone ceiling so far above their bowed heads.

It was all theatrical, cheap and contrived, yet somehow Otto could not shake off a strange sense of fear, as the strains of Wagner's *Siegfried*, piped into the crypt somehow or other, died away, to be followed by the voice of the Führer. It was a recorded speech from the great days of victory, full of bombast, the words as such not saying much, but heady and vital, heavy with the kettle-drum brass of thundering, ranting invective that had once had the blood of his listeners boiling with emotion, their hearts flowing and overflowing with passion, their nerves tingling electrically.

Even now that hoarse Upper Austrian voice still had its effect. As the last words died away, that sombre black crowd which filled the crypt burst out into that triumphal animal, atavistic cry of the old days: '*SIEG HEIL . . . SIEG HEIL . . . S I E G H E I L!*'

A long echoing silence followed, as that voice continued to rant, as it rose to the highest reaches of the crypt, before it finally vanished into nothing. Otto, as mesmerized as the rest, each one of them wrapped up in his private cocoon of memories of past glories, shook his head – hard – like someone desperately trying to wake up from a nightmare. Next to him the Count stood open-mouthed, staring at the wall from which the sound had come, as if he had seen a vision presented there. Otto dug him fiercely in the arm. 'Watch it,' he hissed angrily. 'Don't get frigging carried away *now*!'

It was the Count's turn to shake his head. 'Sorry, Otto. It was just the sound of that . . .' He shook his head again and did not complete his sentence.

Ahead of them, where the *prominenz* stood, heads bowed, hands folded in front of their bellies, as if they were still deep in their devotions, Heinrich Himmler swept back his ankle-length cloak to reveal his skinny chest, devoid of all decorations save the 'Sports Medal in Bronze, Third Class for the Over-Forties'. '*Volksgenossen, Kameraden, Offiziere*,' he broke the heavy silence with the usual formula, 'Folk-comrades, comrades, officers' . . . 'The holy voice of our beloved and great leader, Adolf Hitler, you have just heard will always remain in our minds and hearts. For all time! Then soon our Führer must go from this world, depart this vale of tears, for the Valhalla of the Aryan Warrior.' Himmler let the thought sink in, head bowed momentarily in pious silence. 'We, his loyal thanes, must, however, fight on, continue his great work, ensure that his historic name is never forgotten, that it will transcend the centuries. But how, with our enemies pressing on us from all sides, manipulated by those Bolshevik Jews in Moscow, Washington and London?' He answered his own question immediately. 'We must do so in secret. Already new resistance is springing up behind the backs of the enemy in the territory they have temporarily occupied on the holy soil of the Third Reich. Time and time again our brave Werewolves have struck down those who have aided the enemy. Some of them have died.' Himmler shrugged carelessly. 'What matter? Losses can never be too great. They sow the seeds of future greatness, comrades.'

Under his breath, Otto cursed. Wasn't it always the same with these big shots? They let the damned silly young hotheads do the fighting – and dying – for them, but when their turn came to go, it was usually done nice and comfy in a warm bed. 'Pious sly bastard,' he cursed to himself. 'He'll croak between the shitting sheets just like the rest of the shitting golden pheasants!' But for once, Otto Stahl was wrong.

'So, comrades,' Himmler was saying, 'while General Pruetzmann here,' he turned momentarily to a fleshy-faced SS general, who looked decidedly unhappy for reasons known only to himself, 'continues the fight behind the enemy lines at the head of his vaunted Werewolves, I, your *Reichsführer*, will devote myself to the task of restoring the Reich's military might. In forty-eight hours, I shall leave my beloved Wewelsberg – alas, perhaps, for ever.' Himmler laid his head on his shoulder sadly like a plastic doll with a broken neck. 'Soon, those of you who survive the coming assault might find me in strange company and wonder if even your own *Reichsführer* has gone over to the enemy.'

Sternly Himmler held up his finger, as if in warning. 'Do not fear, dear comrades,' Himmler's voice quivered suddenly with almost unbearable emotion, 'I would gladly fall on my sword here and now, as did our brave Aryan warrior forefathers, rather than betray the holy cause of National Socialism. No,' his voice rose again and grew harsh and hard, in a poor imitation of that of the Führer bringing one of his ranting, confused speeches to a close at the annual Nuremberg Party Rally, 'if you see me with the Anglo-American enemy, with their General Eisenhower, who is incidentally of prime German stock, for example, I will be there for one purpose and one purpose only – to further the cause, to ensure that the battle against the heathen Slavic hordes from the East continues! You, comrades of the field divisions, will fight to the last on the battlefields of the Reich, my young friends of the Werewolf will do so in secret, striking from the night, while I, your *Reichsführer*, will make the supreme sacrifice, give myself to the hated enemy, in a desperate attempt to make him continue the struggle – with Germany at his side.' Himmler's eyes rolled upwards, as the tears streamed down his flushed face, the veins at his temples distended an ugly purple, his woman's hands clenched fiercely, as if he might fall into an epileptic seizure at any second. Otto hoped at that moment that the pious, cunning sod would drop dead in a fit.

But that wasn't to be. 'Comrades,' Himmler roared, his voice hoarse and cracked now with so much shouting, the sweat mixing with the tears so that his face looked as if it had been greased with vaseline in the flickering light of the oil-lamp, 'we continue the fight! You must have faith – and if we do not succeed, we shall drag half the world down to destruction with us, leaving no one to triumph over a defeated Germany! If we do go down, we will take the world with us – *a world in flames*! *SIEG HEIL!*'

As Himmler leaned back, supported by an ashen General Pruetzmann, who clearly did not like the role that had been allotted to him one bit, the crypt exploded in hoarse fury, as the SS officers stamped their feet together, eyes gleaming fanatically, thrusting out their right arms in that old, familiar, hated salute, and roared back, as if they could not wait to see a 'world in flames': *'SIEG HEIL . . . SIEG HEIL . . . SIEG HEIL.'*

Suddenly Otto felt very sick . . .

FOUR

'The pious shit's gonna do a bunk, that's what he's gonna do!' Angrily, Otto spat into the wet, glistening pre-dawn grass.

'Do you really think so, Otto?' the Count asked, as he huddled there in the chill air, waiting for the Mosquito to appear. 'He seemed very genuine to me. He even wept. I was rather moved.'

'You'll be frigging well moved – by the toe of my boot in a minute!' Otto snorted, angry at the Count, the Amis, Himmler, the whole stupid war-torn world. 'Carry on the fight, my holy arse! Himmler's gonna let those silly sods get their turnips blown off on the battlefield, fighting for a cause that is already shitting well lost, while he buggers off with the loot to South America or somewhere.'

'But he said something about General Eisenhower,' the Count objected a little desperately for, good-hearted innocent that he was, he always liked to believe the best of his fellow human beings.

'Eisenhower, even that drunken frigging actor who plays the general[1], wouldn't touch Himmler with a bleeding bargepole! Let's face it, Count, when it comes out what we have done to German-occupied Europe over these last six years, not to mention that dirty business with the Yids, as soon as you mention you're a German, they'll send you to that place where the piss freezes before it hits the deck.'

'You mean Siberia, Otto?'

'Yes!'

'Do you really think that the Western Allies will take this Hitler thing so seriously after they have beaten him?' The Count paused and cocked his head to one side to listen. But there was no sound, save that of the breeze in

[1] See *Otto and the Yanks* for the amazing story of Eisenhower's double.

the trees and the hooting of some distant night bird. 'I mean, they know that we Germans are a cultured people, Otto. Beethoven, Schubert, Goethe and Schiller – all that sort of thing.'

'Fuck that old bunch!' Otto snorted coarsely. 'Once the Western Allies have finally conquered us, all they're going to be thinking of is characters like Hitler, Himmler and Heydrich. We Germans are going to be bad news for the next century or more, mark my words. The land of poets and thinkers,' he added scornfully, 'has become the land of judges and hangmen in the eyes of the world in 1945. They'll have us down with our hooters in the crap for the rest of our days. No, Count, the only thing that smart people like ourselves can do is to vote with our feet.'

'Vote with our feet?' the Count echoed, bewildered.

'Yes, bugger off somewhere else. And to do that, Count, we need Marie . . . the green . . . the filthy rags . . . in short, *money*!' Otto snapped, a note of near despair in his young voice. 'That's why we've got to set up the Amis, get Himmler and his black gang out of that castle up there, find the loot and bugger off . . . at the double . . .' He stopped abruptly.

From the west there came the faint drone of an airplane engine. Swiftly, he turned his head to the wind and, hardly daring to breathe, listened hard, his eyes narrowed to slits. Yes, there it was! There was a plane up there all right, flying very high and at low speed; he could tell that by the note of the engine.

'Do you think it is them, Otto?' the Count asked eagerly.

'We'll soon find out,' Otto answered, and pulled out the J-E. 'Here we go.'

According to Colonel Ersenbrick, at their briefing back in the Rhineland, the J-E or 'Joan-Eleanor' had been invented by the Britishers, and it enabled an agent on the ground to talk directly to a specially equipped plane flying overhead at as much as thirty thousand feet. Since a J-E weighed only four pounds and used small long-life batteries, it was easier to transport and conceal than the usual radio-transmitter used by secret agents, and its high-frequency and vertical cone-shaped directivity virtually defied enemy DFI[1]). The danger of mistakes in transmission was minimized, too, by having the agent on the ground in direct two-way voice communication with the man in the plane, who could request repeats or clarification on confusing points and in his turn give the agent spot briefings. Most important of all, a volume of data could be exchanged in a few minutes which might take days or weeks of periodic normal W/T transmission.

Now, somewhere above the two friends, a specially equipped British Mosquito bomber, built solely of wood and unarmed, but tremendously fast, was cruising, the J-E operator crouching in the tail section waiting to make contact.

Otto pressed his button. The dial glowed. In a whisper, eyes fixed on the velvet sky, he gave his call-sign. 'Here Sugar-plum . . . Here Sugar-plum . . . Come in, Fairy . . . come in, Fairy, please.'

'The Sugar-plum Fairy, get it?' Ersenbrick had said enthusiastically, giving them the secret call-sign. 'Kinda cute, don't ya think? It's the title of a piece of music by . . . er . . . Beethoven, I think.'

The set remained obstinately dead, as the Mosquito droned round in another lazy circle high above their heads in the darkness.

'God in heaven,' Otto cried angrily. '*Where the fuck are you, Fairy?*'

Suddenly, startlingly, the apparatus cracked into life. 'Here Fairy . . . Here Fairy,' a faint voice called and, even at that distance, Otto could hear the disgust in that far-off American's voice. 'Hell, here is Fairy . . . What a cruddy name. Over!'

Otto wasted no time. Germany might be in ruins, but the Gestapo were still active enough. For all he knew the transmission had already been picked up by one of their wireless-detector vans. 'Hello, Fairy,' he said swiftly.

[1] Radio direction finding.

'Located Black One, I repeat, have located Black One. Over.'

'Excellent . . . excellent . . . So the big cheese is there after all? . . . Over.'

'Yes, have seen him personally. Can vouch for the identification . . . According to my information, Black One will remain here for a further twenty-four hours. Over.'

For a moment the set was dead, then the unknown American flying high above their heads in darkness said, 'Okay, here's the deal. Big Friends in Limeyland,' he meant the Flying Fortresses of the Eighth Air Force based in England, 'will come visiting at twenty hundred hours tomorrow night. Got that: twenty-hundred hours? Over.'

'Got it,' Otto replied hurriedly. Already, to the east, the sky was beginning to flush a dirty white. Dawn wasn't far away and he didn't want to be caught out here in the open by some farm labourer going to work or the like.

'All right, swell. Now Sugar-plum, what kind of preparations will you make for the Big Friends so that they'll know – the blind bastards – where to, er, drop in? Over.'

'A blazing arrow, Fairy,' Otto answered, thinking on his feet, 'pointing due north-west . . . er . . . right at Black One's little shack.' Under his breath he muttered, 'That's what you think, Ami.' He continued, 'I shall light it to welcome Big Friends as soon as the local sirens sound. Over.'

Otto could almost feel the unknown American considering his suggestion. Desperately he willed him to accept it; it was vital to the plan. It would be essential if he were going to flush Himmler out with his loot. 'Okay, let's do it like that, Sugar-plum. Blazing arrow pointing due north-west. Roger, and by the way, the chief sends you both love and kisses.' The American operator gave a kind of metallic chuckle. 'Over.'

'Fuck the chief!' Otto cried hotly, but the little transmitter was dead already and above them they could hear the drone of the Mosquito change to an urgent roar, as if the pilot couldn't get out of German air space quickly enough.

Gloomily Otto began to pack up the set, as the noise of the plane died away to the west. 'Lucky bastards,' he snorted. 'Going home to bacon-and-eggs and good coffee, a bleeding nice warm bed – and, for all I know, a nice piece of warm gash inside it as well.'

'But it's been a long night for them, too, Otto,' the Count said in his usual daft manner. 'I think they deserve it.'

Otto rose to his feet and knocked the damp grass from his knees. 'And you deserve a boot up yer stupid ass. Come on, let's see where we can get our heads down till tonight, before the frigging chaindogs spot us and start asking awkward . . . questions. *Los*!'

Without waiting for the Count to move, Otto hid the set once more and set off, shoulders bent, almost as if in defeat. Frowning a little, the Count followed. He supposed his young friend was in one of his usual moods, but then he told himself working-class people are never at their best in the early morning. They were always very moody till they'd had their first schnaps and beer of the day at their 'second breakfast' around nine. It was probably very hard to be working-class . . .

Just over a hundred miles away at the US forward air base at Rheinberg, Captain Moishe MacTavish was coming to that very self-same conclusion.

As he staggered, stiff-legged and partially deafened from the Mosquito, still clutching the precious top-secret J-E set, into the barracks which housed the enlisted men, there seemed to be frauleins in various stages of undress everywhere. The barracks was filled with their giggles, excited screams and the eager squeaking of rusty bedsprings.

'Say, Corporal,' MacTavish snapped a little grumpily at the OD corporal, 'don't those guys of yours know they're not supposed to fraternize with the Krauts? Ike's forbidden it.'

The long-faced NCO looked up from the *Yank* magazine he was reading, combat boots firmly fixed on his desk. 'They don't want to fraternize with them, Captain, they want to fuck 'em!' he answered dourly.

'But they could be fined, even get sixty days in jail, according to the new orders from Supreme Headquarters.'

The corporal shrugged his skinny shoulders easily, long face unimpressed. 'So what, sir? Getting his ashes hauled is the only thing that makes life worth living for your ordinary working-stiff.'

Moishe MacTavish gave up. 'Okay, now where's your signals office? I've got a top priority signal to make – and I'm authorized, Corporal.'

The noncom jerked a dirty thumb down the corridor. 'Along the hall, second door on your right. Staff Sergeant Rizzi's on duty. Ask for him and show him ya ID.' He yawned and bent his head to the magazine once more, plaster floating down from the ceiling, obviously dislodged by the hectic activity up above, onto his balding skull like the first snow of the winter.

Just outside, the signals officer, a PFC standing with his slacks around his ankles, was drunkenly waving his member at an equally drunken blonde, minus her skirt, the two of them laughing uproariously. Moishe MacTavish frowned. He knew the Army Air Corps was slack, but this was going too far. He couldn't get into the signals office with his all-important message for Ersenbrick with the two of them barring the way. 'Hey, soldier,' he cried, 'what the Sam Hill do you think you're goddam doing?'

The PFC turned, a hand still on his dangling member, a bemused smile on his drunken face, while the girl continued to laugh helplessly, tears of joy running down her cheeks. 'Button . . . button came off my flies . . . sir,' he stuttered drunkenly. 'Not what you might be thinking, sir. Miss Adelheid here has volunteered to sew it . . . on agen for me . . . Only we can't seem to find the . . . the needle.' He winked hugely at the blonde.

'Oh for crying out loud!' the captain said in disgust and pushed by the swaying soldier angrily.

Rizzi, dark, unshaven, sucking an unlit cigar, deep bags under his black Italian eyes, was laboriously unrolling cigarette ends and placing the tobacco in a big GI can in front of him on the desk. He was obviously preparing the stuff for the German black market.

The sight annoyed Moishe MacTavish even more. 'Listen, Sergeant,' he snapped, 'there is a guy outside your office minus his pants, wagging his dong at a drunken Kraut fraulein.'

Rizzi's look did not change. 'That'll be Lacey, the drunken bum,' he announced almost pedantically, 'I've warned him already about that blonde. *Veronika Dankeschon*, that's what we call her, VD for short . . . She'll give him the pox yet.'

'Sergeant,' Moishe roared, exasperated beyond all measure by these drunken, fornicating, sullen, enlisted men, 'haven't you ever heard of *non-fraternization*?'

But all the irate officer got for his pains was virtually the same answer he had received from the surly OD corporal. 'Sure, but it ain't much fun being a working-stiff, sir. A little bit o' pussy is all yer average guy can look forward . . . to.'

MacTavish gave up. He pulled out Colonel Ersenbrick's telephone number. 'Okay, Sergeant, I want you to get me this number at once . . . Priority Number One.'

'Sir,' Rizzi took it without interest. 'And who should I say is making the call, sir? They'll want to know at the main switchboard.'

Just in time the dark-faced little officer remembered Ersenbrick's warning to maintain top security at all times. 'In this business, MacTavish,' he had lectured the other officer, more than once, 'it is no names . . . no pack-drill. Yer never let yer right hand know what yer left hand is doing.'

'Say that Fairy –' MacTavish blushed furiously at the name, 'is calling.'

Rizzi took his dead cigar out of his mouth and winked

very deliberately, a knowing smile on his unshaven face. 'That figures – *honey* . . .'

MacTavish could have brained him with his black market GI can.

FIVE

From far, far away to the west, came the first faint dread wail of the siren, sounding its urgent warning. Otto cocked his head to the wind blowing across the blacked-out plain. There was no mistaking it. It was the air-raid warning all right – the alert. The Ami bombers were on their way. As if to confirm his reasoning, another siren mounted on top of the local village school took up the warning. Now, everywhere in the path of the approaching air gangsters, the radios would have ceased their normal programmes and would be broadcasting the details of the advancing armada, the commentators making educated guesses at where they might strike. Otto hoped so at least; for he knew up at the castle, now shrouded in darkness, Himmler would have his people listening, too. Once they heard from the radio that the *Ami Terroristen* had begun to circle, their usual tactic as they formed up to bomb, they would conclude that Schloss Wewelsberg was their target this night and they would panic. Otto prayed that he was going to be right. Everything depended upon a panic-stricken flight from the castle.

He swung round on the waiting Count, as the first flak began to fire, illuminating the sky to the west and the Christmas trees. The huge bundles of flares dropped by the bombers started to float down, glittering, indeed, like an illuminated Christmas tree on Christmas Eve when the presents were given out. 'Here they come, Count, light the arrow.'

The Count reacted at once. Even he realized the danger of their position now. If they were caught lighting a beacon for the Americans the local farmers would beat them to death or they'd be shot out of hand. He lit the paper taper with his cigarette lighter, dipped it in the bone-dry straw that they had been collecting all evening from the abandoned pig-farm which, unknown to the Americans, was going to be the Eighth US Air Force's main target this night, and jumped back hastily as it began to burn.

Rapidly, fanned by the night breeze, the flames swept all along the hundred-metre length of the straw arrow. In an instant the heat was terrific and the flames were leaping high into the air, turning night into day, illuminating Otto's tense, strained, upturned face as he waited for the first sign that the Amis had spotted the marker.

It came almost immediately. He caught a glimpse of a dark spotted four-engined plane, which he knew was the marker plane on which all the rest rallied when a target had been identified. Next moment a great glittering Christmas tree began to sail downwards, like a blazing chandelier falling from the elegant ceiling of some great house.

'They've bought it, Count!' he yelled above the ever-increasing drone of many engines, as the Flying Fortresses started to fly towards the marker ship and its flare. 'They've shitting well bought it! Come on, let's hoof it. Quick.'

The Count needed no urging. He knew the power of the American Air Force of old. The abandoned pig-farm was going to be wiped off the map in a few minutes' time. Hurriedly, he swung himself on the back seat of the rusty tandem that they had looted from the farm that evening.

They set off for Schloss Wewelsberg, while behind them the mighty roar grew in frightening intensity, as one hundred four-engined planes, manned by eight hundred highly trained officers and noncoms, burning up thousands of dollars' worth of gas for every minute they flew, prepared to pulverize an abandoned pig-farm, worth the equivalent of three cartons of *Lucky Strike* (without filter) currently in black market currency.

Panic reigned in the Schloss. Officers raced back and forth yelling orders and counter-orders. Whistles shrilled. Burly NCOs doubled across the cobbled courtyard pulling on their helmets, waving rattles. From the car park and the motor pool there came the sound of motors being started up, and heavily laden servants staggered towards the big Mercedes bearing the departing SS generals' luggage.

General Sepp Dietrich's big open Horch swept by, with the little Bavarian crying, angrily, as his driver hooted his horn to clear the way for his departure. 'Like a Jewish whorehouse . . . *meschugge*, the lot of them! Glad to be going back to the front.'

The first stick of American bombs went down far over on the plain and Dietrich's car shot round the corner and disappeared in a cloud of dust.

'It's working, Count!' Otto hissed delightedly, as they pushed their way through the terrified throng leaving the castle while there was still time. 'It's shitting well working . . . they're shitting bugging out.'

The Count did not speak; he couldn't. In his eagerness to get at the loot, which Himmler had stowed away in his private quarters, Otto was setting a cracking pace. At this rate, he might well have a massive heart attack, the Count told himself, gasping for breath like an ancient asthmatic. He wasn't as young as he had once been. Otto did not notice. He pushed on, shoving officers and civilians to both sides brutally, eyes sparkling with greed and excitement.

Reluctantly, the Count followed. He could never understand Otto's concern with money. He supposed it was something to do with Otto being working-class.

Himmler made his decision at last. As, outside, the guns thundered and the bombers of the US 8th Air Force roared in yet again to plaster the abandoned pig-farm with bombs, he rose to his feet. His breath fogged a little on the icy-cold air of the crypt as he stared around at those who would accompany him on his flight. They were the elite of the elite, the toughest and finest of his SS bodyguard, not a man of them less than two metres tall. 'Comrades, soldiers,' he announced, 'I have made my decision. We take a dive!'

'A dive!' the big men with their hard scarred faces echoed like the chorus in an ancient Greek tragedy.

'Yes. I would not have believed it if I had not seen it with my own eyes. That burning arrow.'

'The burning arrow!' they repeated as one.

'Deliberate sabotage,' Himmler said bitterly, and added a moment later, staring through his pince-nez with sudden tears in his eyes, 'with only one purpose – to murder *me*!'

'Murder the *Reichsführer* SS!' the chorus echoed in shocked tones.

'Yes. It is the work of their General Eisenhower. The raid has been staged to assassinate me – and from that, one can draw only one conclusion. The Western Allies have no need of our German expertise in fighting the Russian subhumans. Mentally unstable, nay mad, as they are, comrades, they are only concerned with the battle in the West, while red hordes swarm through Eastern Europe, taking what they wish. One day, of course, they will learn what a terrible mistake they have made; then they will need us. But till then, comrades, we must survive. Is that clear?'

As one the giants clicked their heels together and bellowed, faces wooden, eyes fixed on an imaginary spot somewhere above Himmler's skinny right shoulder, '*Klar, Reichsführer*!'

'Good,' Himmler waved for them to relax. 'Now we take our dive. Hermann,' he ordered the oldest of his bodyguard. 'The shaving soap, hot water and my razor. I will now commence my disguise.'

Hermann hesitated a moment, genuine tears in his bright blue eyes. 'Not the moustache, *Reichsführer* – not *that*!' he choked, a note of absolute despair in his voice. 'No!'

'*No, Reichsführer*,' they pleaded as one. 'Not the moustache!'

Himmler held up his hands for silence and then stroked his straggly, thin moustache for the last time. 'We all have to make sacrifices for the Holy Cause of the Fatherland. If I must do it, then I must. It will have to go. Hermann, if you please.'

Reluctantly, his legs moving terribly slowly, as if they were hung with lead weights, the blond giant moved towards the stove in the corner of the crypt, where the kettle rested on the green tiles. The preparations for the celebrated dive of *Reichsführer* SS Heinrich Himmler had commenced.

The two of them pressed themselves against the cold stone wall behind the arras, listening with beating hearts to the sound of the heavy boots echoing down the corridor till it died away altogether. Now the only noise came from the bombers at the other side of the plain. It seemed as if the great castle was deserted.

Otto decided to take a chance. 'Let's not waste any more time, Count,' he whispered, awed a little by that heavy echoing silence, 'just in case those Ami fly-boys get lucky and drop a bomb on Wewelsberg.'

'You don't think they would, Otto, do you?' the Count quavered.

Otto grabbed his arm and lugged him from behind the ancient wall-carpet. 'Let's not stay around to find out, eh. Come on.'

The two of them set about systematically searching the upper rooms of the castle in that part of Wewelsberg that Himmler had set apart for himself and his special guests. They were great grey caverns of places, filled with heavy, hand-carved, peasant furniture, painted green and adorned with red hearts, of the kind that the Nazi *prominez* favoured, each room adorned – inevitably – with the self-same portrait of Hitler: the Führer as a knight in armour, mounted on a white nag, and carrying a great blood-red banner bearing that hated crooked cross. Yet each bedroom remained obstinately bare of loot. Ceremonial daggers, encrusted with imitation diamonds, pistols covered with gilt, SS cloaks heavy with rabbit fur masquerading as ermine, were everywhere, as if some crazy thespian had gone wild and had looted the local theatrical outfitters. But there was nothing of any value among the cast-offs of the dying regime.

'Himmler's room,' Otto hissed, pausing at the heavy oak

door bearing the *Reichsführer*'s personal coat-of-arms, which he recognized from that night in the crypt. 'It has to be in here, Count. It has to *be*!' he repeated almost desperately as, far to the west, the first sirens started to sound the 'all clear'.

They thrust open the door. In the flickering light of the great candles, which were the room's sole illumination, it was not hard to determine that this was indeed Himmler's room. There were photographs of the pasty-faced, bespectacled little man everywhere, inspecting troops, meeting Hitler, throwing bits of bread to starving Red Army prisoners cooped up behind a barbed-wire fence, as if he were feeding wild animals at the zoo. 'You tackle the desk, Count,' Otto ordered. 'I'll have a look-see at these cases. Now get on with it, while we've still got time.'

'Yes, Otto,' the Count answered dutifully, and started to open the drawers of the big baroque desk.

The first case, open like the rest of Himmler's suitcases, as if they had hastily rifled for particular items, was filled with old books, most of them with motheaten leather bindings. Otto went through them, nose wrinkled in disgust at the smell they gave off, like that exuded by unwashed feet that had been encased in marching boots for too long. 'Shitting books!' he cursed to himself. 'People spend too much shitting time reading as it is . . . Bad for them!' Angrily, he tossed an old book onto the floor. It gave a clunk, as if the binding might contain some metal or other, as it hit the floor.

Three days later a former student of Yale, masquerading as an infantryman in the 83rd Infantry Division, with more patience than Otto, would recognize it for what it was and quietly slip it into his combat jacket, not one bit worried by the smell. Forty years later that most valuable of medieval manuscripts, the Gospels of Henry the Lion, the Duke of Saxony, and Himmler's hero, would be auctioned off at Sotheby's for nearly three million dollars. But by that time Otto would have engineered his own coup, which probably brought him twice that amount in the sale of world rights.

'It could be in here,' Otto said excitedly, as he spotted the briefcase, bulging with something or other, and still locked unlike the rest of the cases. 'Here, Count, give me a hand . . . Open it!' He heaved the heavy leather case up into the air and, while he held it thus, a red-faced Count strained to open the stiff lock.

Finally he managed it and Otto's face fell when he saw what the briefcase contained: sheaves of paper, covered in pedantic writing, which could only be Himmler's. 'Look at this, Count,' he snorted in disgust, picking up a little grey notebook filled with lists of items, each page initialled in red and the words: *Found to be correct and tallied, week-ending* . . . 'His shitting wife's weekly housekeeping account!' he exclaimed. 'And this. His repayments on his mortgage! Holy strawsack, and those were the kind of shits who ran Germany for the last twelve years. Can you imagine that old drunk Churchill checking his missus's grocery accounts?'

'They were rather a petit-bourgeois lot, Otto,' the Count said. 'I always told Father Christmas that my father would have turned in his grave if he'd have known that I was associating with . . .' He stopped abruptly.

Otto wasn't listening. Instead, he was staring at the picture of a prettyish young blonde he had pulled out of the briefcase, which bore the legend: *To Harrykins with eternal love from his own little Gertrud. Christmas 1942.*

'What is it, Otto?'

By way of reply, his young friend whistled softly and said, 'You wouldn't have thought he would have had the blood in him for a bit of the old mattress polka, would you?'

'What?'

'Why, don't you see? Himmler was sticking his bit of shrivelled-up salami into her – his frigging *little Gertrud*. Look at this.' He held up the half-finished letter which was next to the photo. 'It's from his nibs personally. I'm beginning to recognize the handwriting now. "My own sweet little mummy," ' Otto read out the words, face contorted with disgust. 'What crap! Enough to make yer puke.'

'But do you think we really should read it, Otto?' the Count asked, a worried look on his face. 'After all, it *is* a personal letter.'

Otto silenced him with a look that could have killed, and read on. 'How unfortunate we were not able to continue the act of love the other night . . . He means a fuck, Count.'

His friend winced and closed his eyes. These working-class people like Otto simply had no scruples. The morals of a monkey, the lot of them.

'But in my dreams, my beloved, I have already transmitted the juice of life to my dear Gertrud which is the source of all creation and know that she will be delighted . . .'

'Otto,' the Count broke in, sudden fear in his voice. 'There's somebody coming.'

'What?'

'Yes, listen! Coming in this direction.'

Otto heard the heavy footsteps and knew that their time was at an end. Otto's vision of treasure in the form of gold coins and bundles of American greenbacks vanished immediately. There was no mistaking the harsh sound of jackboots on stone. Only the SS marched like that – and the SS were dangerous, damned dangerous. 'Let's go,' he hissed. 'Through that side door there. It leads out into the other corridor.'

The Count needed no urging. His fleshy, handsome face suddenly pale with fear, he headed for the door, while Otto stood there as if undecided for a moment longer. What instinct made Otto seize that photo and that sickening, half-finished letter, he could never explain afterwards. But he did and, in retrospect, it proved the wisest movement of his whole long, confused career in that Old War.

Five minutes later they were outside once more, hidden in a grove of pines, watching the stream of black Mercedes and Porsches containing their high-ranking SS passengers leaving the castle for good, the faces of the occupants pale and preoccupied in the reflected light coming from the burning, shattered, abandoned pig-farm.

'It's the end,' Otto said miserably. 'They're hoofing it and we'll never find that loot which will put us on the green twig for the rest of our days. *Shit*!' Angrily, he slammed his fist against the trunk of the nearest tree and yelped at the sudden pain.

The Count patted him sympathetically on the shoulder. 'Never fear, Otto, one day, sooner or later, we'll land on that celebrated green twig of yours. But for the time being, Otto, remember this, as the poet once said. "Our business in life is not to succeed, but to continue to fail in good spirits", eh.' He beamed encouragingly at his friend. 'Now what do you say to that?'

But Otto Stahl was so downcast at that particular moment that he did not even have the energy to suggest to Count von der Weide that he should engage in a physically impossible act of sexual perversion with himself . . .

SIX

'The colonel will see you now, sir,' Staff Sergeant Rocock said in an exhausted voice and leaned suddenly against the wall, as if he might faint at any moment.

Captain Moishe MacTavish looked at the haggard, young noncom with the dark circles under his eyes and what looked like cotton wool protruding from his flies. 'Aren't you feeling well, Sergeant?' he asked. 'Don't you think you ought to see the medics?'

'I'll be okay, sir,' Rocock said gamely, raising himself from the wall by an effort of sheer naked willpower. 'It's all this night work, sir . . . keeping the Red Ball rolling with supplies . . . for the guys at the front.'

Moishe frowned. Why was there cotton wool hanging from his flies and what was the Kraut broad up the hall doing with her mouth?

'Does that German woman know you, Sergeant?' he asked a little severely. 'She seems to be making sort of . . . *kissing gestures*.'

'What, sir?' Rocock turned, his emaciated face suddenly ashen with fear. 'Oh, my God,' he gasped. '*The Dracula of Dueren*!'

'The what . . .'

But Staff Sergeant Rocock was already stumbling away down the corridor, one hand stretched out in front of him like a blind man, calling over his shoulder in a fearful voice, 'Got to go, sir . . . The boys at the front, you know . . .'

Moishe MacTavish shook his head and told himself, if the German army had failed to defeat the Yanks, it looked as if the frauleins were now going to do the job for them. He knocked at Colonel Ersenbrick's office and counted off the standard ten seconds which the fat bastard always made everyone under the rank of bird colonel wait until he barked his customary, 'Come!'

'Not at this particular moment,' he sneered to himself, and opened the door. Clicking to attention and feeling like something out of a John Wayne western, he saluted and called, 'Captain M. MacTavish reporting for duty, sir!'

Normally old 'Hairy Prick' was pleased by the formula; it reminded him, he was wont to say with a smile, 'of the good ole' days before this goddam war started and you could get some real soldiering in'. But not today. His face remained as grim and threatening as always when he was wearing his 'war-face, number one', that is, *Snafu*, or 'situation normal, all fucked up!'

'Sit!' he commanded and without any further ado, barked, 'Those two goddam Kraut cruds have double-crossed us.' As always when things went wrong, Ersenbrick used the plural. When he was winning, it was always that singular 'I'.

'How exactly, do you mean, sir?' Moishe asked carefully.

'How exactly do I mean?' Ersenbrick bellowed. 'Why in Sam Hill's name, air recon this morning showed that Wewelsberg Castle is completely intact, but deserted! The goddam fly-boys bombed some farm or other. The inspector-general has ordered a goddam inquiry, too.'

'But the flaming arrow, sir,' Moishe protested.

'Fuck the flaming arrow!' Ersenbrick beat the table with his clenched fist so that the canteen cup of coffee in front of him trembled alarmingly. 'They damn well set us up. For all I know the bastards bugged out with Himmler himself. God damn it! The war's nearly over and here's my only chance to get that first star before it is, and now those cruddy Krauts go fucking things up for me. For crying out loud, MacTavish, ain't they got any heart, not one little iota of compassion!' For one awful moment, Ersenbrick's ruddy face seemed to break up like a soft-boiled egg hit too hard by a spoon, as if he might well burst into tears at any moment.

But West Point triumphed in the end. Colonel Ersenbrick fought back his tears bravely and ordering himself mentally to 'brace', threw back his shoulders and tilted up his chin, as if he were an eighteen-year old cadet again. 'So it seems that the top SS brass has already bugged out of the damned castle. In other words, Himmler is still alive. Now there is still a slim chance that we can get him, MacTavish, if we play it smart.'

'Yessir,' Moishe answered, a little worried about that use of 'we'. Was it the 'royal we' of the kind that the top brass delighted in; or was it the real McCoy?

'You see, it seems there are two escape routes still available to the top Nazis trying to take a powder.' Ersenbrick rose and strode over to the big wall map of North West Germany. 'While those damned little Werewolf kids keep on murdering for their Führer, there's one group of their bosses, trying to do a deal with us up north around the Hamburg, Copenhagen, Lübeck area.' He made a swift circle with his hand over the towns, 'And there's another bunch of the mothers running for their lives down to Bavaria and Austria – here – where the Krauts are supposed to be putting up their final last-ditch stand at the Alpine Redoubt.'

'Sort of Custer and the Seventh Cavalry thing, sir?' Moishe suggested helpfully and wished, next moment, he hadn't.

Colonel Ersenbrick fixed him with a cold look. 'There is *absolutely* no comparison, Captain,' he snapped. 'For those of us who studied at the Point, General George Custer,' he said the names, as if they were in separate italics, 'is a gentleman and a hero. It was unfortunate about those damned Indians not realizing that General Custer's strategy was aimed at achieving something else. In fact, my class of thirty-four always thought the Indians were damned unfair. Clear?'

'Clear, sir, absolutely,' Moishe snapped back, telling himself he had enough trouble on his hands with World War Two to be bothered about fighting the Battle of the Little Big Horn.

'Now,' Ersenbrick continued. 'Intelligence reports that Himmler is one of their big shots who has been trying to do a deal with the Western Allies. So my educated guess is that he is now heading north up to Flensburg in the province of Schleswig-Holstein, where the Kraut admiral – Doenitz – is in command.' He indicated that Moishe should come to the map.

From outside Staff-Sergeant Rocock's broken, quavering voice penetrated into the suddenly silent room: 'Give me a day off, please, *schnuggi* . . . just a couple of hours of rest . . . I c . . . can't stand any more of it. *Schnuggi* . . . *No!*' It ended suddenly in a cry of almost animal despair.

Moishe MacTavish bit his bottom lip with worry. Those goddam frauleins ought to be arrested and flung into the goddam stockade. With all that free nooky about, it had to be sheer hell for the average GI; you couldn't just keep that kind of thing up for long on C-rations.

'Well, as I see it,' Ersenbrick continued, 'while General Hodges' First Army is plunging deep into Thuringia – here – and General Patton's Third is barrelling along through Bavaria towards Austria, covering scores of miles a day, this guy Sir Montgomery and his Limeys are sitting on their keesters on the left bank of the River Elbe – here – just below Hamburg, probably drinking that warm piss they call tea and eating goddam crumpets as well, for all I know! Anyway, Sir Montgomery is going to do the Second Battle of El Alamein all over again. Christ on a crutch, ever since 1942 he has been fighting that goddam African battle over and over again! You know the setpiece crossing of the River Elbe. Big artillery barrage, commandos, paratroops, the whole shoot. It's gonna be D-Day all over again, MacTavish, you know.'

Moishe MacTavish *did* know. He had jumped with the US 101st Airborne Division into Normandy on D-Day and had been part of the mess at Ste Mere Eglise. He had jumped again in the Arnhem fiasco and that hadn't been much better, with another third of the division going to the cleaners. After that, and being surrounded with the reformed division at Bastogne in December 1944, he had decided that if he was going to survive this war, he'd better get out of the goddam 'Screaming Eagles' pretty quick. On

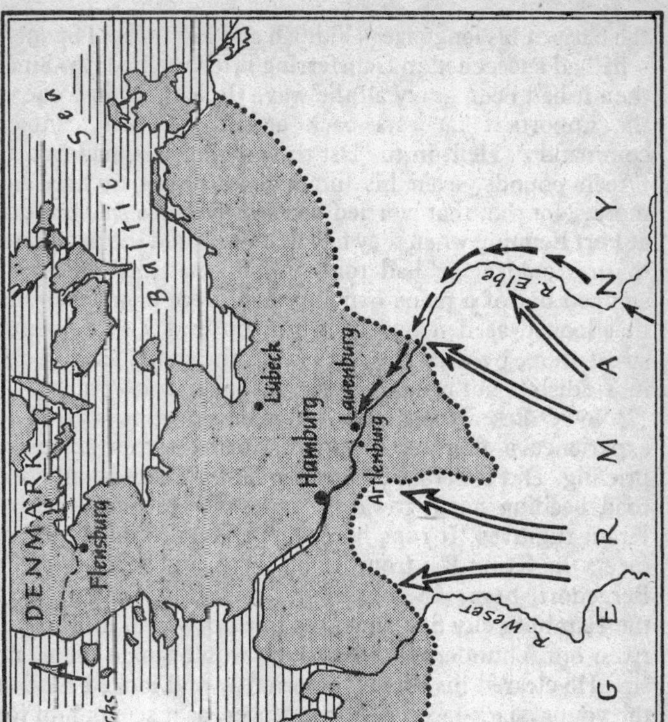

THE SITUATION IN N.W. GERMANY, APRIL 28th, 1945

the basis of his language – Yiddish and high school Spanish – he had succeeded in transferring into Intelligence. Since then it had been gravy all the way. He had become one of the important fat cats back at base, a real 'canteen commando'. Hell, in the last three months he had put on fifteen pounds, even his jump boots didn't fit him any more. Not that that worried him. Right since the first day at Fort Benning when they had demonstrated the parachute to the rookies, he had told himself that any man who stepped out of a plane hanging on a piece of knicker silk that looked as if it had been run up in a Third Avenue sweat-shop, by what the old Jewish emigrants used to call in Yiddish 'a hot needle', was ripe for the trick-cyclist.

'Now,' Ersenbrick went on, while Moishe started to experience a faint sensation of alarm at this extensive briefing. Did it herald danger for him? 'There is only one road heading north towards Schleswig-Holstein open to Kraut fugitives. It runs here, to Lauenburg on the Elbe, meets the Kraut B-4 from Berlin there, and heads towards Bergedorf, here, where it comes under the protection of the Hamburg city flak guns, the most powerful in Europe. Even our Thunderbolt whizz-kids won't tackle them, no sir!' He cleared his throat importantly and looked hard at the young, dark-faced airborne officer, as if seeing him for the first time. Suddenly Moishe felt the first, faint stirrings of apprehension. Regular brass never noticed a guy until there was trouble brewing. Was there trouble brewing for him, he wondered with abrupt fear?

'So if Himmler and his party, on their way to *Gross-admiral* Doenitz, take number four up to, say, Bergedorf, before making a run for it for the north and Flensburg, where the admiral is, what would be the best spot for us to stop them? Eh? Where could we do it the most efficiently?'

There he was, going on about that 'we' again, Moishe cursed to himself. He could have groaned out loud. Instead he said, 'Where indeed, sir?'

Ersenbrick beamed at him as if he had said something important. 'You've seen it, haven't you? Why, here, on the far bank of the Elbe at Geesthacht. Road narrow there, flanked on one side by the steep bank of the Elbe and the other by some wooded heights, with no side-roads leading off down which they could bug out. The perfect site for an ambush.'

'An ambush, sir,' Moishe echoed warily, a cold finger of fear tracing its way down his spine slowly.

'Yes. The Limeys have agreed to lend me a troop, of what the hell do they call them, of their commandos. They're gonna go in with the first wave across the Elbe at a place called Artlenburg – here. Their mission is to avoid being bogged down in the actual fighting – there's a whole Kraut division defending the other bank – and whip up to the heights beyond, head due west and set up the ambush on Route Number Four just outside Geesthacht.' He sat down suddenly, as if exhausted, his fat chest heaving. 'Captain MacTavish, you will be in charge of those commandos and I don't have to tell you the importance of your mission. Bring in Himmler and I get my first star. For you, there'll be the Silver Star.'

Moishe MacTavish was too shocked to tell him he already had the decoration, in triplicate. In a voice that he hardly recognized as his own, he heard himself asking, like a condemned man inquiring about his final breakfast before they took him to the electric chair, 'And when do I go up, sir? . . .'

Ersenbrick forced a weary smile. 'That's the style, MacTavish. Bully for you! The Ladies from Hell – and all that kind of crap. You Americans of Scotch descent can't get enough of combat, can you? I guess it's the wild Celtic blood and all that. Good booze, you folks back home make, too. A swell native brew!'

At that particular moment, Moishe MacTavish, whose father had changed his name from Finkelstein to MacTavish, the day he'd gotten out of the garment trade and moved to Scarborough, New York, and made his application for the local golf club, which was lousy with prejudiced goys, would have willingly given ten silver stars for one big glass of that celebrated 'native brew'.

Outside an unutterably weary voice, which belonged to

the frail shadow of the one-time 200 pound Staff-Sergeant Rocock, was saying, '*Schnuggi*, I don't think I can make the stairs to my bunk . . . I think you'd better give me a hand.'

Moishe MacTavish nodded his head in sad, silent agreement. He knew only too well, just how the poor clapped-out bastard felt . . .

He'd need a stretcher to get out of this room. *Veh, O Veh*, now the shit had really hit the fan. Moishe MacTavish was going back to the frigging war again!

SEVEN

For nearly a week Montgomery's Second British Army had been dug in on the bank of the Elbe waiting for the order to attack. By now all of the soldiers, down to the humblest private, knew that this would be the last great battle the British army would fight in World War Two, at least in Europe. 'We're the ferking BLA[1] ain't we, mates. Get this little lot over and then it's Burma looms a-ferkin-head!' They would assault the river, the last water-barrier in the heart of what was left of Nazi Germany, between the fishing villages of Artlenburg and Avonsdorf, and establish a bridgehead, some 2,500 yards wide, centred on the village of Schnakenbek on the other side. Once they had penetrated the enemy positions to a depth of 1,500 feet, the armoured divisions would pass through and race for the coast at Lübeck. Now, as April 1945 neared its end, the commandos and the Scottish infantrymen of the 15th Scottish Infantry Division, who would be making their third major river crossing under fire of the campaign, prepared for the assault. The enemy wasn't aggressive. Indeed, civilian boatmen still plied their trade in the no-man's-land in the middle of the Elbe in full view of both sides. Ferrymen jokingly offered to take the British across for twenty pfennigs or one Woodbine. But the bandy-legged, young, tough Glasgow infantrymen who held the bank on the British side suspected that the ancient Elbe sailors, in their black peaked caps and moleskin waistcoats, were pulling their legs. All the same they flung the ration 'coffin nails' at the grinning old farts and told them what to do with their oars, which was something that was patently impossible.

It was thus that Captain Moishe MacTavish found the British army in those last days of April. As his jeep rolled

[1] The British Liberation Army.

across the flat countryside of the Vierlanden market-garden area behind the Elbe, he saw them everywhere, housed in the red-bricked, half-timbered German houses, which they shared with the civilians and their animals, cleaning their rifles and Bren guns for the umpteenth time, brewing up 'char' or frying bully beef over their little 'tommy-cookers', or simply sitting in silence on wooden benches, smoking their coffin nails and staring into nothing, like men who were enjoying one final period of contemplation before 'it' started once again.

On one occasion his progress was stopped by a huge crowd of silent soldiers, their helmets removed, leaning on their rifles, so that they looked like youthful shepherds, listening to a sharp-faced man, whose hard, beaked nose lay in the shadow of the floppy black beret he wore. Moishe recognized him at once. Hadn't he seen him virtually every week in the newsreels for years now? He was too far away to catch all of what the little man said, but bits and pieces came floating over in his direction, as he waited without impatience to be on his way. 'We're here to win . . . That's our job . . . Never put my chaps into battle unless I know they're going to win . . . Sure we're going to win this one . . . We've winning material . . . and we're the winning team . . . We've got two thousand guns, . . . we've got over one thousand and fifty tanks . . . we've got nearly a thousand aircraft . . . we've got . . .'

'Throw in a ferkin case of ferkin pale ale for me, Monty,' a corporal with a bronzed face who had the look of an old soldier about him said cynically, 'and I'm with yer, mate.' But no one was listening to cynics this day. All eyes were fixed on the dynamic little man in the floppy black beret standing on the bonnet of the jeep.

'Now I'm going to let you in on a little secret, chaps . . . My plan . . . all very straightforward, not too complicated . . . Pick a little bit of good ground . . . say about three or four hundred yards of enemy front . . . Knock the stuffing out of it with the guns and the bombers . . . Pour in the armour . . . and then finally when the fighting and the danger is all over . . . send in you infantry chaps to mop up . . . Done it before, Africa, Italy, France . . . going to do it here soon . . . Knock the old Jerry for six, what . . .'

It was all over. A fart of a red-capped staff officer, all gleaming brass, white blancoed belt and monocle, took off his cap and called, 'Thwee cheers for Field Marshal Montgomewy, chaps . . . Hip, hip . . . Hoowah!'

In spite of the staff officer's absurd, affected appearance, the young cannonfodder of Montgomery's army responded with a will. A tremendous cheer rent the still afternoon, which sent the crows rising from the skeletal trees, cawing in hoarse protest.

A few moments later the little man was on hand, his aides tossing out tins of ration cigarettes to left and right, as the khaki ranks of excited infantrymen parted to let Montgomery's jeep through.

'Gonna be a bleeding cake-walk . . . Monty never loses . . . Well, he's not like the rest of them generals, at least, full of piss and vinegar, allus going on about yer blanco and how many studs yer got in yer bleeding boots . . . War'll be over in a week . . . What a turn-up for the bleeding books . . .' they said.

As he waited for them to drift back to their billets, their young faces flushed and excited, those who had managed to grab one of the cans of cigarettes he had tossed to them exhibiting them proudly to their mates, Moishe wondered at how they believed Montgomery. The little field marshal had sold the coming battle to them like a Fuller's brush salesman, with his foot in the door, selling a brush for the john to some dum-dum of a housewife. He shook his head in wonder. There were a lot of smart cookies in New York who could learn a lot from the cocky little Britisher with the floppy beret. When he was finally able to drive on, he started to feel a little better. Perhaps it wasn't going to be another Ste Mere Eglise after all.

Captain 'Red' O'Dare, the commando troop commander, whose right cheek was scored by a terrible dull-red scar, which looked like the work of a drunk armed with a blunt can-opener, was not as sanguine as his commander-in-chief.

As he and Moishe squatted in the shell-shattered ruins of one of the fisherman's cottages that lined the Deich at Artlenburg, staring through the growing shadows at the steep, wooded opposite bank of the Elbe, he said, 'The bugger's three hundred feet wide at this point, ye know, and the current's at least five knots. Not to mention the fact that the Hun's got at least a battalion of infantry waiting for us at the other side.'

Moishe swallowed hard. 'At your battalion headquarters they told me they're an ears and stomach battalion. All cripples who can't see and can't eat solid food.'

O'Dare laughed bitterly. 'They would. But the pricks have still got eyes and fingers to pull triggers with, haven't they?' He shook his head. 'It's going to be no walk-over and the boys,' he indicated the men in green berets dug in behind him along the river bank, 'are getting tired, very tired. After all, they've mostly been at it since the Lofoten Islands business.'

'Christ!' Moishe breathed, impressed. 'That was back in 1941, wasn't it?'

'Something like that, I suppose,' O'Dare answered a little warily.

'My God, O'Dare, I was a senior at Colombia still in 1941.' He shook his head in mock wonder. 'You've been fighting all those years. Incredible!'

'Yes, I suppose it is,' Captain O'Dare said mildly and added then, 'Suppose we'd better get some shut-eye before the big show commences, eh?'

'Hell, I couldn't sleep a goddam wink!' was Moishe MacTavish's heated reply.

At eleven o'clock that night it started. 'Inflating parties forward!' officers all along the bank commanded.

Out of the glowing darkness the boat-carriers appeared, stumbling under their loads between the guide-tapes. They unrolled the clumsy rubber parcels which were the assault boats. Hastily, they were attached to the cylinders containing the compressed air. Everywhere they began to hiss. The rubber creaked. Monstrous rubber slugs appeared as if by magic and the carrying crews stepped back hastily, as if in fear. One by one, they slipped into the still waters of the Elbe.

'Secure boats!' the order came.

Stakes were hurriedly secured in the wet sand and the boats were attached to them in groups of four.

Now the assault infantry and the commandos waited tensely, their officers repeatedly glancing at the green-glowing dials of their wristwatches and telling themselves it had to happen soon – it had to!

It did. At midnight precisely, a thousand guns opened up on the British side in a typical Montgomery 'Alamein barrage'. For the last time in World War Two, British infantry in Europe were awed by the sight of a great bombardment and the dramatic crimson fires which started up almost immediately on the German side. At Artlenburg, Moishe and the commandos could now stand upright on the bank in safety, hidden in the shadows, as the sky became as bright as day over the river. Searchlights bounced 'Monty's moonlight' from the clouds. A fantastic pattern of pink stabs and flashes of orange flame erupted across the river. Like man-made forked lightning, the tracer shells swept over the water, dragging their glowing, hissing shadows behind them. Here and there a maverick shell exploded too early, tossing up a ball of fire like a Roman candle. Now the Bofors anti-aircraft guns, used in a ground role this day, pumped white tracer in a diagonal stream across the Elbe. These were to be the guide-lines for the assault force. In a matter of minutes the great river had acquired a lethal and terrible beauty.

But there was no time for the beauty of the scene now for the moment of truth had arrived. The night air was suddenly filled with a droning, ominous roar like that made by a squadron of heavy bombers.

'The Buffaloes!' O'Dare roared into a mesmerized Moishe's ear. 'Won't be long now!'

One by one, the 20-ton amphibious monsters roared out of Artlenburg's main street. They rumbled to left and right alternately. Now they were crawling up the six-foot high Deich, throwing up mud to left and right in a great shower. As one, they splashed ponderously into the water like a school of metal hippos.

'Here we go!' O'Dare bellowed above the ear-splitting racket. 'Into the boats, lads!'

Abruptly Moishe was being carried along with the rest, submerged in a crowd of shouting, sweating black-faced commandos like 'Mister Interlocutor' in a nigger minstrel show.

With startling suddenness, that tremendous barrage lifted and then stopped altogether. It was too dangerous to continue at that range. As Moishe slipped and slithered down the muddy bank, the leaves and twigs lashing and slashing at his face, the Germans took advantage of the pause. Everywhere on the far bank, they rose from their foxholes and gunpits and began returning the enemy fire.

Once again, night was transformed into day, as machine-gun bullets hissed flatly across the water, dragging their white, smoking trails behind them. Long-range cannon barked throatily. Great heavy 88mm shells tore the sky apart, as if they were ripping a tremendous piece of canvas. Behind Moishe on the British bank, huge spurts of flying mud and earth erupted into the air, and suddenly the entire river boiled in white fury as the shrapnel from the exploding shells came howling down.

The assault boats chugged on steadily, fighting the current, rocking violently every time a shell exploded near by, whipping up the water in wild, crazy anger. Captain O'Dare ducked for the umpteenth time and cried yet once again, as the water came slapping down, 'The Hun certainly wants to make clean corpses of us, Captain, that's for certain!'

An ashen-faced Moishe, his mind full of those terrible memories of Ste Mere Eglise, with the dead paratrooper hanging from the burning church steeple and the bell tolling as if for the corpse, clutched his stomach as the little boat rocked yet again violently, and muttered miserably, 'I think I'm gonna be seasick!'

Now the first of the commandos were springing out of their little rubber boats and plunging into the water, ignoring the slugs lashing it furiously on all sides. Effortlessly, not seeming to notice that they were carrying sixty pounds in the rucksacks on their backs, they started to scale the cliff before them. On top German soldiers, easily identifiable in their coal-scuttle helmets, lent over and started to lob stick grenades at the attackers.

'Bugger that for a tale!' O'Dare cried, balancing on a ledge next to a most miserable Moishe. He paused for a moment, raised his tommy-gun, and loosed off an angry burst upwards. The .45 slugs ripped the length of the top of the cliff. There were sudden screams of agony. A German came tumbling down, to hit the ground below like a sack of wet cement and sprawl there, arms and legs outspread in a crimson star of his own blood, head in the water. Abruptly the grenade-throwing ceased.

'Bash on, lads!' O'Dare cried cheerfully, slinging his tommy-gun again. 'Remember yer British!'

'Ay, but do yon buggers up there know that?' a surly voice called back through the glowing darkness.

O'Dare laughed out loud. 'The lads are in great form, Captain,' he announced and pushed Moishe upwards again, straight towards that cliff-top ablaze with the lights that meant sudden death.

Six jets, line astern, came hurtling towards the river. The commandos froze, clinging desperately to the rock face. 'Jet-propelled planes!' O'Dare yelled above the howl. 'The Hun's new secret weapon . . . A new chapter in man's achievement, what?'

'*Fuck the whole fucking book*!' Moishe yelled back miserably, as the Me-262s hurtled downwards, anti-personnel bombs falling in deadly rain from their sinister black-painted bellies.

Men fell screaming in agony on all sides, as the bombs

exploded everywhere among the crowded assault infantry, turning the beach below into a mess of writhing, blood-splattered wounded, their severed limbs scattered all around them like offal piled up, red and steaming, in front of a wholesale butcher's. Then they were gone, zooming high into the night sky, followed by the hopeless cotton puffballs of the too-slow English flak.

O'Dare tugged Moishe to his feet and thrust him the last few paces to the top on legs that felt as if they were made from soft India-rubber. 'Move it, old boy . . . Let's get the job seen to before those Brylcreem boys in their new toys come back.'

All around them, the commandos were crying for some reason unknown to Moishe, who had naturally never heard of Tommy Handley and his famed ITMA radio show, 'After you, Cecil . . . No, after *you*, Claud,' as they pushed each other over the top.

Moishe grunted and dropped to the wet grass. Next to him Captain O'Dare rallied his men. 'To me, lads . . . to me, lads! Rally on me . . .' the words froze on his lips.

Moishe raised his head out of the wet grass and chanced a look. Ahead of him, the night was split by the crazy thrust and stab of small arms fire. Tracer zig-zagged back and forth everywhere like flights of angry red hornets. Another shell exploded in a flash of violent cherry-red – and then Moishe saw it.

Moishe gulped with total, overwhelming fear. A long, low, tracked vehicle was rumbling towards the stalled commandos, crewed by strange creatures, muffled up in thick leather coats and masks, their eyes concealed by thick goggles, so that they looked like something out of the horror movies he remembered from those pre-Pearl Harbor matinées at the Roxy. '*Flame-thrower*!' a commando screamed in a paroxysm of unreasoning terror. '*They're gonna flame us*!'

'Don't panic, lads!' Captain O'Dare called and ran forward, tommy-gun clenched to his head.

'*NO*!' Moishe MacTavish screamed desperately. 'Don't do it, you fool . . .'

Too late! 'Red' O'Dare was crouched directly in the path of the monster, tommy-gun at the ready, waiting for it like some latterday David.

The masked creature behind the nozzle of that cruel, impossible weapon spotted the lone Englishman. Desperately he swung the gun in O'Dare's direction. The commando captain fired off a quick burst. The slugs howled harmlessly off the vehicle's armoured plating. Moishe hugging his body to the wet grass, as if in the embrace of a hot-blooded lover, could hear the *zing-zing* of the ricochets quite distinctly. The flame-thrower operator pressed his trigger. There was the hushed intake of air like some primeval monster drawing a breath. A forked tongue of oil-flecked flame shot out a good hundred yards. The grass hissed and steamed in its path and the air was full of the stink of burning oil. Just short of where O'Dare still stood defiantly, the ground turned a dull glowing purple. The heat was terrific. Even where he lay, a horrified Moishe could feel the very breath being dragged from his lungs by it.

Outlined a stark dramatic black by the dying flame, Captain O'Dare desperately fitted a new magazine to his tommy-gun. But it was already too late. The monster had crawled right into range. That terrible weapon hissed once more. Again that long tongue of flame licked out greedily. Moishe ducked, feeling the hairs on the back of his head beginning to singe. O'Dare screamed, shrill and hysterical, as the flames wrapped themselves around him. For what appeared an age, he seemed to remain standing there, as the flames tore at his flesh, filling the air with the sweet sickly scent of burning meat, until he started to crumple and wither. Finally he was standing there, hunched and crouched, like some terribly shrunken black man, the useless tommy-gun welded to his fingers for all time.

A moment later there was a hollow boom of a PIAT shell[1] slamming into the metal side of the flamethrower. It heeled, as if struck by a sudden tornado. It came to an abrupt halt, a bright silver hole gouged into its plating.

[1] A British anti-tank weapon.

For a moment nothing happened. Suddenly white smoke began to pour in a thick cloud from the stricken flame-thrower. The crew panicked. They attempted to fling themselves overboard before the inevitable occurred. The furious hail of fire from the maddened commandos kept them inside. Next moment the 'mix' burst into flame. In an instant that terrible flame engulfed the screaming, hysterical Germans. Within moments they were consumed by those greedy black-red flames, sinking into that red-glowing steel coffin, charred black, and shrunken to the size of pygmies.

With a great cheer the commandos swept forward, firing from the hip as they did so. Everywhere Germans began to pop up from their holes, like grey ghosts risen from their graves. '*Kamerad*,' they quavered, '*bitte Kamerad*!' Desperately they flung away their weapons and raised their dirty white hands in surrender, throwing blind glances to the night sky, as if they sought God's mercy up there. But this terrible night, God had gone elsewhere. There was no mercy to be found in the glowing, lurid heavens. The commandos plunged into them, striking out with their butts, the toes of their heavy boots, killing and maiming blindly, carried away by the fury and rage of the battlefield.

Numbly, Captain Moishe MacTavish watched them go, still on his knees as if praying, gaze half-taking in the body of 'Red' O'Dare, crouching there in its awesome, charred blackness. Moishe's brain seemed to be working with great difficulty. He couldn't think straight. 'I can't leave him here . . . just like that . . .' he seemed to be saying to himself, the tears streaming down his dirty bewildered face . . . 'Can I, Red? . . . Can't . . . Can't . . .'

'*BUT HOW THE FUCK ARE YA GONNA CARRY A FRIGGING STIFF*?' an angry voice roared in rage from deep within. '*TALK FRIGGING SENSE, MOISHE, WILLYA*!'

Abruptly something snapped within Captain Moishe MacTavish. With a muttered curse, he flung the carbine he had been leaning on, as if on a crutch, away. His helmet followed in a gesture of disgust. Madly, his fingers fumbled with his ammunition belt, as if he could not remove it fast enough. It, too, went flying into the night. For a moment he stood swaying there like a drunk, his breath coming in harsh, hectic gasps. Suddenly he howled at the sky like a mad dog, 'I've had enough . . . enough! Can't ya frigging well understand . . . *ENOUGH*!'

Sobbing for breath, the unheeded tears streaming down his desperate, contorted face, Captain Moishe MacTavish stumbled off into the glowing darkness, away from the sounds of battle and the great injustice. He would fight no more . . .

EIGHT

I met Mr Moishe MacTavish only once. Of course, forty years later he was no longer 'Moishe' but 'Martin', as befitted a well-known New York publisher; and naturally the 'Martin' had been abbreviated to the trendy 'Marty' of our time. Publishers, like bad actors, are always very trendy. It was at one of those publishers' 'bashes' that are held every night during the great annual Book Fair at Frankfurt. As always the fat cats from London and New York were trying to get drunk – quickly – on duty-free whisky, the local *appelwoi*, German *Sekt* – anything that was cheap and potent. After sitting on their pin-striped bottoms at the Fair all day, perhaps it was understandable that they sought oblivion swiftly – and cheaply. Once back home the firm's accountant would go over their expense sheets with the usual eagle-eye and a great deal of sad tut-tutting.

The big hotel ballroom was full of smoke, noise, drunken laughter, and the sound of breaking glass. At publishers' parties, they always break a lot of glasses, especially if they are German glasses and they, the publishers, don't have to pay for them. Up near the stage a fat lady publisher in a silver-lamé trouser suit was trying to organize a game in which a spoon tied to a long tape was inserted down the neck of the participant's clothing and extracted at the bottom, and then passed onto the next participant who would do the same. 'Please no unseemly laughter from the back there, Cooper!' she cried, red-faced and half-drunk, 'and you, Cheetah, take your hands off Jenny's blouse. We haven't started *yet*, you know!'

Here and there, desperate types still huddled in corners, eyes watering behind their horn-rimmed spectacles with the smoke, trying to convince obviously drunk and uncaring publishers to buy their latest blockbusters. For the most part, the publishers simply sat or stood around, working hard at getting drunk before their taxis called to cart them off to their own hotels. As many of them were there on package deals and shared their tight bedrooms with someone else, it was better to be drunk and out to the world by the time they got to bed, than listen to their room-mate snoring heartily all night long. *Male* room-mates, I must point out hastily; for sex rarely takes place at the Book Fair, although most of the publishers drag along a poor little female dogsbody, to fetch and carry, with them. Secretaries in fact, they call themselves grandly 'editorial assistants' and 'report' back directly to the publisher's wife on any 'high jinks'. Hence booze, and not sex, is the soporific at Frankfurt.

Next to me an American, who was fool enough to still be wearing his 'exhibitor's badge' on his lapel like some mid-Western Elk at the annual reunion, was saying, unconvincingly, to a British publisher who wore a polka-dot bow tie, which marked him as an 'old-established' London publisher, 'You see, André, this property is about a hound that talks . . . Yeah, yeah, I know, a dog that goddam talks! . . . But ya've got to unnerstand, it ain't a particularly great year, André . . .'

I was only half-listening and feeling lonely, for authors have no business being at Frankfurt. (The publishers are here to talk money and they don't want scribblers to get in the way of selling the product), when a voice said, 'You're Kessler, Leo Kessler, aren't you?'

I turned and smiled automatically. Publishers like authors who smile a lot; it means that perhaps, for once, they are not going to ask for money.

Opposite me stood a small, fat, bald man, with bright black buttons for eyes, who was obviously very American and very Jewish. 'MacTavish,' he said, thrusting out a pudgy hand, 'pleased to meet you, Leo.'

Obviously he saw the blank look in my eyes, as I took his hand, and added hastily, 'You know, MacTavish . . . Marty MacTavish of "Morlock and MacTavish". Morlock don't exist any more, of course. Went heavy into fibre-diet, jogging, stretching, and all that kind of health crap last year. Mid-life crisis, I guess. Died jogging in Central Park last fall, leaving me his equity. God rest his soul!' MacTavish bent his head in mock piety and folded his fat white hands across his lower body, as if he were afraid that one of the more pansy publishers – and several of the more flamboyant ones were present – might grab his genitals at any moment, if he weren't careful.

I grinned. MacTavish of 'Morlock and MacTavish' was obviously something of a card. 'Naturally, now I know, Mr MacTavish. You do those books about –'

'Yiddische mommas,' he beat me to it with a lopsided grin, 'heavy with *schmaltz* and good advice, who have wayward sons who want to marry *schicksas* and don't want to be doctors . . . and ugly daughters with spots and no periods whom they can't get married off . . . and grumpy old husbands who work in Third Avenue as pattern cutters and are dying of cancer though they're not telling anybody. We do a kinda poor man's Arthur Miller or, even better, Phil Roth – with a happy ending, natch!' He looked up at the smoke-shrouded ceiling with those cunning bright eyes of his, as if thanking God personally. 'Long live the Yiddische momma!' he breathed fervently. 'She's kept me in bagels these many years.'

Now I knew who the little stranger was. His firm was the Jewish-American equivalent of Mills & Boon, serving up romantic lower middle-class New York *schmaltz* for the four million Jews of that great city – or at least for the female half. With the kind of profits he had to be making, I told myself, Mr MacTavish could have bought a whole kosher supermarket, never mind a bagel!

MacTavish waited for the laughter to subside at the far end of the room where a military book publisher, who had once been a well-known amateur rugby forward, had pulled too energetically and had his whole team on the floor, the men grabbing their loins, as if they had just been goosed, the women tugging wildly at their skirts. 'Airy, isn't it?' a drunken art director, who invariably spoke broken German of the 've haff vays of making you talk' type when he was in that condition, cracked, looking up the skirt of a red-faced editorial assistant, who had been trendy enough to not wear any knickers.

'What did yer expect, Patrick,' someone else commented in mock cockney, '*fevvers*?'

'Wrong place for you to be, Leo,' he said. 'Surprised to see you here at all. Authors are poison here.'

'I know. A writer doesn't know what to do with himself at Frankfurt,' I agreed gloomily. 'Publishers just don't want to know us.'

He nodded sagely, savouring his carrot-juice. Obviously, Marty MacTavish was not altogether immune to the current health fad, I told myself. His pockets were probably full of brewer's yeast tablets and halibut oil capsules. Later I could have kicked myself for not having been more perceptive. He was a publisher, too. Why the hell was *he* talking to me, then, in the first place?

But I suppose I was glad that anyone at all had condescended to address a few words to me, and I just swallowed the bait unthinkingly.

'I quite liked that Otto book of yours – the one where he gets entangled with Churchill's supposed illegitimate son,' he said, staring up at me, a smile on his fat face, but those eyes of his as cold, calculating, and as cunning as ever.

'Oh, you mean, *Otto and the Reds*. Thanks. It wasn't bad.'

As an American and a New Yorker, he should have replied heartily with a punch to my right arm, 'Bad . . . hell, Leo, it was *great*!' But he didn't. Instead he said, 'Do you really believe that Herr Stahl did go through all that . . . back in 1940 . . . and all the other things that you've written happened to him during World War Two?'

That '*Herr Stahl*' should have warned me. Why the formality from a sharp cookie like Marty MacTavish? But once again it didn't. As I have said before, I suppose, like most authors, I am hopelessly naive, especially when there is a good story involved.

I explained to him the evidence that Otto had offered me to back up his amazing tales of his life during that Old War and how, in most cases, it seemed to substantiate his claims. 'After all,' I concluded, 'Otto is simply a poor old man living in virtual exile in a crummy Spanish seaside town on what amounts to pennies. He wouldn't have the resources to fake up his stories. I mean, look at the cost to the *Stern* to fake that Hitler Diaries thing this spring! According to the press accounts, it cost the publishers something in the region of ten million marks to set the business up.'

He nodded sagely, obviously convinced – or so I thought then. 'Yeah, you're right, Leo. Your Herr Stahl wouldn't have that kind of dough, that's why I guess we have to believe him, eh.' He took another careful sip of the carrot-juice, and as afterthought, popped four yellow tablets into the mouth. He was into brewer's yeast, after all. 'They nearly got away with it, though, didn't they?' he said after a moment, swallowing the health tablets with difficulty.

'You mean the *Stern* people?'

'Yeah. If the deck hadn't been stacked against them and that Lord guy of yours, the one with the old-fashioned eye-glasses, hadn't backed out, they could have easily doubled their initial investment. Twenty million D-Marks. That's nearly *ten* million dollars.' He grinned ruefully. 'More than *The Schicksa Bride* by Rachel Rubenstein, my latest hit,' he added easily, 'will be earning this side of the twenty-first century.'

'I suppose so,' I answered a little bewildered, wondering where our conversation was leading.

In fact, it led nowhere – *then*.

Suddenly the military book publisher, who had once been an amateur rugby football player, jumped onto the stage with surprising agility for such a heavy man and declared, 'Dance . . . everybody's gonna dance . . . *NOW*!'

The drunken art director turned up the tape recorder to full blast and the whole room was submerged – surprisingly for that trendy gathering – by the 'Blue Danube'. In a flash they were all waltzing gracefully and with tremendous dignity, as if they were *Hochadel* launching out into the first dance of the evening at Vienna high society's traditional New Year Ball.

Mr MacTavish and I stumbled back hastily out of the way and that about ended our conversation. The noise was too great. Thus it was that I nearly missed his last remark. It was – and I swear this is true – 'Say, Leo, does Herr Stahl still have those deep blue eyes?'

Then, at Frankfurt, I was convinced that I had not heard him correctly. How would Marty MacTavish know about Otto's eyes. Now I know, to my chagrin, that I had heard him well enough . . . That evening at that drunken publishers' bash, I had been party to the first phase of the most daring plot that Otto had hatched in his whole long, crooked career . . .

BOOK THREE: THE END RUN

'Mucha musica, pero poca opera.'

An old Spanish saying[1].

[1]Roughly: A lot of music, but little opera.

ONE

The battle for the heights above the Elbe was virtually over now. Boxlike British ambulances bearing the legend 'carrying casualties' were already beginning to rattle and shake their way down to the Elbe once more, to where the Buffaloes waited to ferry the wounded back the way they had come. Long files of cocky little infantry, strung out to the left and right of the road, were beginning to march along the cobbled road that led to Hamburg. Tanks rattled by, splattering them with mud. Important looking officers in stiff raincoats gesticulated with their swagger sticks in every conceivable direction, while others consulted maps. MPs on motor bikes roared back and forth. A spotter plane came zooming in low to drop a message by parachute. Everywhere there was ordered chaos, with the guns already commencing the new barrage to smash the hastily prepared German positions on the Hamburg road.

Moishe MacTavish, helmetless and without a weapon, let himself be carried forward by the throng of cheerful young soldiers in mud-splattered khaki. No one took much notice of him. Even the harassed redcaps, with their slung sten-guns, directing traffic paid no attention to him. Perhaps they thought he was another of the carelessly dressed unarmed war correspondents who were scribbling notes and snapping pictures of 'a typical cocky Jock who has just given the Hun what-for'.

He struggled on, submerged in that cheerful khaki tide, seeing here and there an elderly German man or woman staring at the soldiers in total disbelief, or sobbing heartbrokenly, as if their world had fallen apart which, of course, it had. There was no saving Germany now; the last major natural bastion on the way to Berlin and defeat had been overcome. The vaunted 'One Thousand Year Reich' of Adolf Hitler was doomed.

The sudden, terrifying shriek of an 88mm crashed into Moishe MacTavish's reverie. As one, the marching soldiers threw themselves into the churned-up mud, as the one hundred pound high-explosive shell slammed into the damp fields to the right of the road, throwing up a shower of grass sods and earth.

Moishe lay panting like a stranded cod with the rest, as the fist-sized red-hot gleaming pieces of shrapnel hissed and whizzed through the trees all around, snapping off branches as if they were matchsticks, gouging great white scars in the bark, until a harsh, yet humorous voice cried, 'All right, laddies, the bad, bad boogeyman's gone away now. You can get on yer plates o' meat agen!'

Reluctantly Moishe looked up, as all around him the young infantrymen began to stand up, patting their knees, fiddling with their packs. A big burly MP sergeant stood there, hands on his hips, looking at the soldiers with a half-smile on his tough red face. 'Come on, now,' he urged, 'we've got a date with Adolf. Can't disappoint the old bugger, can we now?'

Moishe MacTavish had seen it all before. The tough sergeant rallying a shaken group of soldiers with the same old mixture of contempt and humour. No wonder they said the non-commissioned-officers' corps was the backbone of any army.

He got up and the MP sergeant noticed him for the first time. He came over as the infantry started to move out once more, took in Moishe's appearance – no helmet, no weapon – and the fact that he was an officer though; therefore, a person of respect and importance, and said, 'Don't think I'd go any further, if I was you, sir,' as he indicated the way ahead with his cane. 'The buggers have got a couple of 88s dug in in that wood at three o'clock. Yon infantry will have to winkle them out before we can press on.' He frowned and stared almost in sorrow at the pale young faces passing them, as they stood there at the side of the muddy road. ' 'Spect some of the poor sods'll buy it before this day is out.' He dismissed them and continued with a note of false cheerfulness in his voice,

'Why don't yer take that lane over there, sir?' he suggested. 'They're setting up Div. HQ in yon farmhouse. Sit it out for a bit . . . Get yer wind back, like.' He touched a bewildered Moishe on the shoulder. 'You being a lone Yank like, sir, I shouldn't wonder if the general don't invite yer to have dinner with him tonight.' His big hand tightened on the other man's shoulder and Moishe found himself turned in the direction of the low, thatched-roof farm, surrounded now by radio cars, light armoured cars and jeeps, with mud-splattered dispatch-riders careering back and forth down the rutted lane that led to the place.

Numbly, his legs feeling as if they were made from soft India-rubber, Moishe MacTavish started to limp towards the HQ, followed by the big NCO's hearty voice, crying, 'That's the stuff, sir . . . Straight on, sir . . . And don't forget to give my compliments to the divisional commander . . . ha, ha! . . . All right, you shower o' shit,' the tone changed to a harsh bark, 'open them there legs and get moving . . . Nothing'll fall out . . . and if they do, Sergeant Simpson'll pick 'em and send them home to yer loved ones . . . *Come now, let's be having yer!*'

Blindly, like dumb animals being led to the slaughter, the heavily laden infantry slogged on towards the waiting guns – *and death!*

Morosely Moishe MacTavish munched a bully beef sandwich, between sips from a mug of scalding hot tea, which one of the cooks had given him saying, 'Real sarnt-major's tea this, sir. Half a tin of evaporated milk to each dixie. This is the stuff the general hissen gets, sir.' He half-listened to the buzz of conversation from inside the farm, while the radios crackled and the typewriters clattered away.

The divisional general looked all of seventy, with his bristling white moustache and eyebrows, but he was a regular old fire-eater, Moishe could see that all right. Curry in his blood and fire on his breath. 'I don't want any damned explanations, my boy!' he was crying at an ashen-faced young major, whose right arm nestled in a blood-stained sling. 'Never explain. Doesn't do in the army . . . Trouble with you young fellers, no damned spirit. *Attack*! That's the only thing to do. Nothing to lose. Everything to gain. Get in among them with cold steel . . . That'll settle Jerries' hash for him . . . *Attack*!'

'Yessir . . . attack,' the major agreed wearily. He saluted awkwardly with the bandaged arm and went out.

The general smiled happily, as if he had achieved something, and bellowed, 'Orderly, where's my bloody char? At the double, man!'

Moishe turned away from the window, as the infantry major splashed through the mud to a waiting jeep. 'Counter-attack, George,' he called miserably to the bare-headed captain behind the wheel, 'that's the good word.'

'Oh, fuck,' the captain said without any emotion, as if it were a fact of life, 'that'll do for the rest of the fucking company. Wonder how long it'll take for my wife to get the widow's pension through?'

Next moment they were off, back to the front, leaving Moishe to stare after them, half-eaten sandwich in one hand, mug of tea in the other. It seemed to him, as he stood there in that busy farmyard, with the guns thundering to the east, that it had always been thus in every army. Those fire-eaters of professional soldiers, American, Limey, Kraut, Wop, even Nip, for all he knew or cared, only made a name for themselves by making a ballsup of things. How else did the troops get their medals for gallantry? Why, because the Old Man had made a boo-boo and the troops had to go out into the flying shit and rectify it. A fight against impossible odds was only possible because the brass made a cock-up of the battle. And there were a lot of brave guys about – some stupid, some without imagination, some patriots – but plenty brave, who didn't simply turn and bug-out, as any sensible person would do. No, they lowered their horns and went straight in like a bull at a gate. They won their medals, mostly posthumously, and the general won his battle – and was given another star.

It was in this gloomy mood that Moishe MacTavish was disturbed by the harsh Scots voice. 'D'ye ken where I can get rid of yon Jerries, mon?' it enquired, full of the bitterness and toughness of the Gorbals (though, Captain Moishe MacTavish, naturally, did not know that). 'Well, mon, dinna stand around like one o' each waiting for the ferkin' vinegar? Where's yon POW cage?'

Moishe shook his head, as if he were having great difficulty in comprehending. The language seemed like English, though he could only make out one or two words. Had English-speaking German shock troops infiltrated the divisional headquarters? It was a favourite Kraut tactic. He turned, his hands half raised. Goddam, why hadn't he destroyed his dog-tag with that tell-tale 'H' for 'Hebrew' stamped on the metal? He'd tell them he was an Italian-American, if they asked. That would explain his dark complexion. Perhaps if he threw in a couple of words of his limited Italian like 'pizza' and 'tutti-frutti', they might believe him. '*Io no parlo tedeschi* . . .,' the Italian died on his suddenly dry lips.

Facing him was a bandy-legged, undersized soldier with a balmoral cocked at an impossible angle on his sandy head, an angry look on his dirty red face, bayonet clutched in his equally dirty hands. 'They're ferkin' well looting the ferkin' cellars up yonder,' he barked in that impossible accent. 'Bags o' smashing schnapps . . . and I'm ferkin' well lumbered with these ferkin' Jerries! . . . Now where's the ferkin' POW cage?' He thrust up his bayonet and his two prisoners stumbled obediently forward, faces showing their relief at being released from the clutches of this bandy-legged little monster.

For a moment Moishe MacTavish could not believe the evidence of his own eyes. It couldn't be!

'Fuckin' SS . . . Ought to have shot the buggers on the spot . . . getting in the way of a bloke and his drink . . . But the company commander wouldna have it, *the soft nelly*!' the little man sneered, while Moshe continued to stare at the two bedraggled dirty prisoners, clad in the uniform of the *Waffen* SS. 'Sez I've got to take them to the cage and bring back a ferkin' signed chitty to prove I've took 'em there!'

Moishe finally reacted. 'I'm an officer,' he said, not taking his eyes off the two Germans, whom he recognized from that day on the barracks square in what now seemed another age. 'I'll sign your . . . er . . . chitty for you.' Hastily he fumbled in his tunic for a piece of paper and a stub of pencil, while the little Scot made a great show of rolling up his sleeve to reveal the half-a-dozen looted wrist-watches tied there and consulting the time, as if he were in a tremendous hurry to be off.

Madly Moishe scribbled on the back of the pack of V Matches. '*Received from unknown infantryman, two officer prisoners. Signed Moishe MacTavish (Capt. USA).*'

The little Scot took the V Matches and read the words, moving his lips as he did so. '*MacTavish*,' he said finally, looking at Moishe's eager dark face suspiciously. 'Ye dinna look like no ferkin' MacTavish to me!'

'The New York branch of the clan,' Moishe replied hastily. 'It's all that sun over there . . . Gives the family a darker colour.'

The Scot shrugged. 'Ah, weel, if ye say so. Then I'll be off.' A moment later he was running down the track, as if he could not get to the looted schnapps quickly enough, leaving the three men standing there in heavy silence, broken only by the steady boom of the nearby guns.

Moishe MacTavish listened attentively while Otto told his story, pausing only to take a bite of the bully beef sandwich which the little American had given him. At his side, squatting in the cover of the undergrowth behind the farm, the Count nodded occasionally, as if happy that his young friend had finally recovered from his mood of black despair. He, too, felt a sense of overwhelming relief. When those little bandy-legged soldiers had winkled them out of the cellar up the roof, for a few moments he had felt that his end had come. There had been a cross-eyed one at the back of the mob who had clamoured all the time, 'Give 'em to me, mates! I ain't croaked a Jerry yet on account of me bleeding wall-eye – and the ferkin' war's nearly over.' There had been a note of despair in the youngster's voice. 'Go on, lads, gie a little un a chance, will yer!'

But the tall, chinless officer in the long bedraggled skirt which reached down well below his knees would have none of it. 'That's enough, Jenkins!' he had commanded. 'SS officers . . . probably possess vital information . . . Must get them back to Intelligence . . . at once . . .' The officer seemed to have difficulty uttering more than four or five words at one go and his skirt kept threatening to slip from his skinny hips at any moment. All the same the Count had been grateful to him; he had undoubtedly saved their lives. Now, it appeared, they had been caught up in the Great Game yet again. There was still hope.

'So, you see, Captain MacTavish,' Otto concluded, 'we were out for the loot. Only something went wrong. Himmler had hidden it,' he shrugged a little helplessly, 'but not where we had anticipated.'

Moishe nodded understandingly. 'It's Murphy's Law, Herr Stahl. If a thing can go wrong, it *will*. But you see, you did make a great mistake.'

'What?' Otto asked, wondering why this little Jew should be interested in their affairs. They were Kraut prisoners-of-war, who were lucky to have missed a sudden death. Of what interest could they be now to the victors, especially if that victor was Jewish to boot?

'You didn't ask Himmler personally where he stashed away his loot,' Moishe answered with an easy smile, a plan starting to unfurl in his mind like a lazy, heat-drugged snake shaking out its coils. 'The only guy who is going to tell you where the dough is – if there *is* any dough, and I agree with you, Herr Stahl, that there is some – is the *Reichsführer* personally.'

'But why should he tell me, Captain?' Otto objected. 'I'm just an ordinary chap. Of no importance to a big animal like that.'

'Not big animal, but big *shot*,' Moishe corrected Otto's

English automatically. 'But you see, Otto – may I call you Otto?'

Otto nodded, his bright blue eyes staring at Moishe's cunning dark face in bewilderment.

'Well, Otto, it's Himmler's turn to become a nobody. His days of being a big shot are over. *We're* the big shots now.'

Otto shook his head. 'Captain . . .'

'Call me Moishe.'

'Moishe, I don't follow.'

'Listen, Otto,' Moishe said urgently, the plan becoming ever clearer as he spoke. 'You and me, and the Count here as well, have taken our licks in this fucking war. And what will we get for it? Nix! A drawerful of cheap medals, made of tin, not much better than the toy G-man badge I wore as a kid in knickers.'

Otto wondered if his new-found Jewish friend was some kind of pervert. But perhaps, in America, boys did wear knickers. He dismissed the intriguing possibility and concentrated on Moishe's urgent words.

'But we didn't stick our necks out all these years for peanuts, Otto. We want more out of it. If Himmler has stashed away some loot, why should it go to the US Treasury? Why shouldn't the guys who did the fighting get their share?' He nudged Otto knowingly. 'After all, we were the guys who got the shit flung at us . . . So, Otto, how about this as a deal? We team up. You and the Count know what Himmler looks like and you're Krau . . . excuse me . . . Germans. I'm an American officer with the know-how and the muscle. I think the Limeys have got North Germany tied up. There's no escaping for *Reichsführer* SS Himmler. Soon or later he's gonna turn up, when they all start surrendering. And when he does,' Moishe MacTavish looked from the Count and then to Otto and back again, 'we're gonna nobble him, the three of us.'

Otto and the Count looked at their new-found friend, still puzzled. 'But why, Captain . . . er, forgive me, *Moishe*,' the Count asked, 'do you want us to work for you?'

'*Jawohl!*,' Otto agreed. 'A Jew and two Germans. That is, if you'll forgive the plain German, not exactly a shitting ideal combination this month.'

Moishe shrugged easily. 'Who cares? All I care about, Otto, is getting my greedy little pinkies on Himmler's dough and making my own separate peace with the fucking world. Now what do you guys say?'

Slowly and solemnly Otto nodded his head and stuck out his hand. 'You're on, Moishe. Let's make our separate peace with the fucking world!'

Almost as if to symbolize the significance of that decision, a truckload of British infantrymen rolled back, the young soldiers bawling lustily, as they moved towards the new battle and what awaited them up there, '*For we're saying goodbye to them all, the long and the short and the tall . . . For yer'll get no promotion this side of the ocean . . . FUCK 'EM ALL, THE LONG AND THE SHORT AND THE TALL . . .*'

And then they were gone, that long drawn-out, contemptuous 'fuck' trailing behind them until it vanished for ever . . .

TWO

The big SS officer dropped, panting, into the wet grass, as the burst of machine-gun fire swept the length of the river bank, ripping up angry little bursts of mud. To the right of the bridge a mortar opened up with a thick *crumpy* grunt and mortar bombs howled obscenely from the dawn sky. Great holes appeared in the field to the left of their hiding place like the work of gigantic moles. Himmler, or Sergeant Hitzinger, as he was now calling himself, ducked swiftly as the earth pattered down on his helmet like rain.

The big SS officer from his bodyguard didn't seem to notice, but then, Himmler told himself, *he* had been at the front right from the start of the war. The soldier had an unfair advantage over someone like himself who had been forced, by circumstances beyond his control, to fight his war from a desk in Berlin, eating his heart out to be with his brave fellows in the line.

'*Reichsführer*,' the officer suddenly barked, 'the only way we're going to get across is by a straightforward frontal attack. There is no time now for the usual flanking attack. It's right at them, like Blucher. If we don't make it within the next thirty minutes, we'll never make it. The Tommies are bringing up more troops all the time. Well, sir, what is it to be?'

Himmler's single eye (for he had hidden the other with a black patch so that he looked something like a stage pirate) flooded with tears. 'Oh, my brave fellows, what can I say?' he sobbed.

The big SS officer had no time for histrionics now. Those Tommy slugs were getting damned close and once they had ranged in their mortar, he told himself, well then it was good-night Maria, sleep tight – *for shitting ever*! 'All right, sir,' he snapped. 'Frontal attack it is. You,' he barked at the one-armed young lieutenant, carrying a

Schmeisser, his belt filled with stick grenades, a belt of extra ammunition draped around his neck, 'you the walking arsenal. You come with me. We'll tackle the bridge. The rest of you, except you and you, will come up ten metres behind him – well spread out, remember. You two,' he indicated the two men he had mentioned, 'you are responsible for the *Reichsführer*'s safety. And I'll have the eggs cut off'n yer with a blunt razorblade, if you make a cockup of it. Clear?'

'*Klar, Hauptsturm*,' they echoed as one, their breaths fogging on the cold morning air.

The big soldier gave his band of desperate men one quick look of appraisal and, evidently liking what he saw, snapped, 'Right then, you heroes, what are you waiting for? Now it's march or croak, remember!'

'March or croak,' they cried in that hoarse, tough manner of the frontline SS. '*Reichsführer*, we go!'

Himmler straightened himself up as best he could in his present condition. 'God go with you, my brave chaps.'

'Hell, God,' someone sneered. 'He left Germany a long time ago. We're not going to get much out of God this shitting day.'

'You'll get the toe of my dice-breaker[1] up yer fat fart-cannon in a minute, if yer don't hold yer water,' their leader grunted, shoving a stick-grenade down the side of each tall jackboot and then unslinging his machine pistol. 'Right, move out.'

Himmler opened his mouth to speak, but he was too overcome with emotion to do so.

Watched by a mesmerized Himmler, who was seeing real combat for the first time in six years of total war, the veterans moved to the attack. They proceeded in hectic little bursts of energy, taking advantage of every depression, cluster of bushes, every shell hole, the early morning mist curling up greyly about their crouched bodies. Opposite them, on the other side of the river where the Tommies were dug in, all was silent. There was no sound save for the hoarse crowing of the ravens in the skeletal trees which

[1] Slang for the soldier's jackboot.

fringed the bank. For some reason they had suddenly stopped firing.

Himmler dug his manicured nails into his hands, painfully, with tension. He knew this was their last chance. If his brave fellows could not break through here and escape into the no-man's-land that still lay to the south, he was trapped. It would either mean surrender to the decadent Anglo-Saxons, and he knew that they would never deal with him, or that last bullet to the brain. His SS *had* to break through this dawn. He wouldn't be able to bear the shame of surrender.

Up front, the *Hauptsturmführer* had crawled almost to the bridge itself, and still the Tommies hadn't detected him. Now his men were spreading out in a rough, thin skirmish line to left and right of the bridge, waiting there for the signal from their leader. There was still no sign from the other side of the river that the Tommies had spotted the SS. Their positions remained obstinately silent. Himmler hardly dared to breathe. How exciting combat was! Why had it taken him so long to find this out, he asked himself? There was something heady, almost intoxicating, about it. He felt his heart racing like a crazy trip-hammer. Next to him, the two giants left for his protection licked suddenly parched lips and looked at each other in glum silence. Himmler did not see the look. His whole attention was concentrated exclusively on the men at the river bank.

With startling suddenness, it happened. The *Haupsturm* was on his feet, in full view of the unseen enemy, shouting, running, zig-zagging like a football player from left to right, as he doubled towards the bridge, Schmeisser clutched tightly to his right hip.

'*Alles fuer Deutschland!*' his men shouted crazily as they stumbled into the river, weapons at the ready. '*Es lebe unser Führer . . . Sieg Heil . . . SIEG HEIL!*'

Himmler could have fainted with the delicious ecstasy of the sight. How brave . . . how beautiful . . . were his young giants, as they plunged and stamped through the knee-deep water, crying their bold slogans, fresh faces carried away by the fevered excitement of this tremendous moment!

'Who the sodding hell goes there?' a startled voice called in English from the other side of the bridge. 'Don't yer know the ferkin' war is over, yer silly sod?'

The SS pushed on, the words not understood.

'I'm telling you there's a ferkin' ceasefire!' the angry voice of the unseen Tommy continued.

'Alles fuer Deutschland!' the sweating, red-faced giants cried in sudden triumph. The Tommies weren't firing at them. As usual the buck-teethed Englishmen had pissed their pants. They were going to surrender. *'Alles fuer . . .'*

'Alles fuer fucking Churchill!' the angry English voice yelled and then in sudden alarm, 'the silly buggers haven't read Part Two Orders, lads, they're at it for real. *OPEN FIRE!'*

A flare hissed into the grey foggy sky above the river. Crack! It opened with a snap of explosive. Red light gushed forth. Himmler groaned. In an instant everything below was bathed in a blood-red, glowing eerie light. Almost immediately, the British line erupted into violent life. Tracer started to cut flatly across the water, right into the line of the advancing Germans.

On the bridge the giant *Hauptsturm* ran on, weaving to left and right desperately, as the bullets whipped up vicious little spurts of blue flames at his flying feet. Yet he seemed to bear a charmed life. The slugs missed him by inches. A wildly contorted face under a soup-bowl helmet loomed up. The SS officer pressed his trigger. The Schmeisser chattered frantically at his hip. It took all his strength to hold it. The Tommy reeled back screaming, the blood seeping a bright red through his tightly clenched fingers where he held them to his ruined face. Another Tommy sprang up from a hole to the right of the bridge. The *Hauptsturm* hadn't time to fire. The man was already levelling his rifle, face set and determined. He lashed out with his cruelly nailed boot. The Tommy screamed and reeled back, spitting bright white teeth out of the red gore which had been his mouth. *Hauptsturm* Heinrici laughed out loud with triumph. He had nearly done it. He was nearly across. *'Mir nach, Maenner,'* he called, *'Mir . . .'*

He gasped with sudden shock, as the burst of machine-gun bullets caught him right in the stomach, ripping the flesh to shreds, knocking the wind out of him so that for a moment he simply stood there, choking and gasping for breath like a boxer caught by a surprise blow to the solar plexus. He shook his head angrily. The mist in front of his eyes stubbornly refused to clear. Something wet and warm was creeping down the front of his body. It seemed to take him a long time to summon up the strength to look down.

A grey-purple serpent, which steamed evilly, was beginning to creep out of the red gore of his shattered stomach and tumble down to his knees to hang there in steaming, pulsating obscenity. He groaned. He staggered on for a few paces, dragging that monstrosity with him, and then the final burst ripped the length of his body from head to toe and he was momentarily galvanized into violent action, flung from side to side before he was smacked against the side of the bridge-head.

Below, in the water, the excited English infantry were slaughtering the rest of the attackers, their blood dyeing the running water red, as they threshed and turned in their final agony, fighting to the last to keep on their feet. To no avail. One by one they went under, their screams turning into a choked gurgle as the water flooded their lungs, and they were carried away by the current.

Himmler watched aghast, in open-mouthed amazement. 'Is it . . . always like this . . . in battle?' he asked in an awed, small voice. 'This . . . *slaughter* . . .?'

One of the big men guarding him looked at the dead bodies floating rapidly downstream and said bitterly, 'Always, *Reichsführer*. Or did you think the enemy handed out peasoup and hot sausages to our lads at the fr –'

His companion punched him hard in the upper arm. 'Hold yer trap, Hans,' he grunted. 'No use – now.'

Across the river an angry voice was shouting, 'Cease-fire . . . for Chrissake, will yer stop firing . . . They've had it . . . *And the bloody war's fucking well over, ain't it?*'

Although Himmler knew no English, even he could note the horror in that lone voice, though the words meant nothing to him.

Slowly, the firing died away, until there was one last rifle shot like the sound a twig makes when it cracks underfoot in a wood on a dry summer's day. A long, brooding silence followed and seemed to go on for ever.

On the bridge the dead *Hauptsturm* still stood upright, propped up somehow by one of the girders, his blood dripping steadily to the ground. In the water the last of the slaughtered SS were drifting away lazily, face-down in the stream, grey-clad rumps sticking up a little absurdly, as they vanished beyond the trees.

'There ain't no more of the silly sods!' a voice called suddenly and made Himmler start. 'The rest of them must have buggered off, Sarge.'

'Go and have a dekko on the other side, Charley,' another voice ordered. 'You go with him, Peters – and you, you lazy sod, Smith, Seven-Five . . . and watch yer bloody step. Yer never know with the old Jerry!'

Himmler peered out of his one eye at the bridge. A cautious figure, bayoneted-rifle held across his khaki chest, had appeared at the far edge of the bridge. Behind him were two other Tommies, both holding their weapons at the high port, as if ready to use them at any moment. Himmler chuckled softly with excitement, the horror of a few moments ago forgotten now. 'We shall take them, men,' he hissed and fumbled for his pistol holster.

Hans caught his hand just in time. '*Reichsführer*,' he hissed urgently, 'no!'

'But why?' Himmler protested, unable to move in the big man's vicelike grip.

'Because we ain't got a shitting chance,' the other guard said bitterly. 'The clock's in the pisspot for good, Himmler!'

Himmler was too shocked by the man's tone to do anything but gasp again and then, after he had recovered himself, ask in a suddenly subdued voice, 'But what are . . . we going to do now?'

'This!' the angry one cried. He grunted and ripped off his officer's stars to fling them far into the bushes.

'What *are* you doing, man?' Himmler protested.

But already the man who had torn off his badges-of-rank was rising to his feet, his big hands held high above his head, a servile smile suddenly on his face, as he quavered, '*Nix schiessen, Kamerad . . . nix schiessen . . .* We friends . . . Look,' he held up his right arm higher so that the sleeve fell back to reveal the wrist-watch tied to the wrist. 'Looki-looki, tick-tock for Tommy!'

That did it. The spell was broken. The three Englishmen slung their rifles as one and were running forward excitedly, the one in the lead crying, 'Bags me the watch, 'cos I'm a frigging corporal – and rank hath its privileges . . . It's mine!'

For one long moment, as the excited Tommies pelted towards them, Himmler did not know what to do. His world had just fallen apart. Now even his SS idols had betrayed him. Suddenly the man who had once terrorized three hundred million Europeans from the Urals to the Channel was at a complete loss what to do next.

'Help me,' he croaked miserably, 'help me, please . . . I don't really feel very well . . .'

Hans took pity on his former master. As he pulled off his own stars and tossed them, together with his pistol, into the bushes, before he, too, surrendered, he hissed out of the side of his mouth, 'Throw away the pea-shooter, put up yer hands, and keep your trap shut . . . *Here the buck-teeth bastards come . . .*'

THREE

'I maintain, gentlemen,' the fruity voice came wafting out of the open window, as Moishe braked the car to a halt, 'that fornication with a nice bit of German crumpet isn't fraternization, no sir!'

'And how do you work that out, Jumbo?' another voice queried good-humouredly.

'Well, it's just fornication, isn't it? I won't use the other four-letter word, in case the padre here goes red –' there was a burst of hearty laughter. 'As long as you keep your cap on and your weight on your elbows, it's simply sex, not love. *Ipso facto*, not fraternization, gentlemen.'

Again there was laughter and someone said, 'I say, Bimbo, you'd better tell that one to Monty. See if he'll buy it.'

Moishe eyed Number One Interrogation Camp a little anxiously. It was like all the camps he had ever seen since he had first arrived in Europe, courtesy of the US Army.

A couple of acres of absolutely bare earth (the prisoners always ate up any vegetation within reaching distance, including grass) surrounded by tangles of nine foot high concertina wire, broken at intervals by stork-legged wooden towers, equipped with the same old emergency searchlights and bored machine-gunners, smoking moodily, occasionally shouting the odd joke to their nearest comrade, and waiting for their spell of duty to end. Inside there were the same old aimless prisoners in their dirty grey overcoats, walking around in slow circuits, mostly in groups, chatting in a desultory fashion. Here and there he saw the odd looney, the one who was obviously heading for a breakdown in the immediate future.

'Nice day for the shitting salt mines,' Otto sneered in the back of the requisitioned German Mercedes. 'Great crap on the Christmas tree, how many more of these dumps have I to go into?'

Moishe, at the wheel, didn't answer. As for the Count, his soft heart went out to his shabby starved countrymen, dangerous SS criminals that they might be. Defeat was terrible. He knew, for instance, that if he were to throw the butt of the cigarette he was currently smoking into that cage, there would be a riot. Men who had once commanded battalions, perhaps regiments, officers and officials who had had the power of life-and-death over whole cities, major provinces, would fight and claw to be first to get a drag at that unbelievable gift that had so suddenly fallen into their midst. These days, the average German would kill a fellow German for a pack of *Lucky Strike*.

'All right,' Moishe broke into the heavy silence, as he prepared to leave the car for the gate, where the white-blancoed sentries eyed them suspiciously, 'you know the deal? We're from the CIC, looking for war criminals who have taken a dive. You, Otto, are our stool pigeon. You, Count, are the representative of the Swedish Red Cross.'

'*Tak, tak*,' the Count agreed, adjusting his armband with its Red Cross insignia, and falling into his role as easily as he had always done. '*Ja*, I am from Sweden . . . to help our poor unfortunate German brothers.'

Moishe shook his head in mock wonder. 'For Chrissake, Count, don't get carried away! Those guys inside that cage would murder their own lawful mothers for a pack of cigarettes. They are war criminals. Okay, we've done it before. It's very simple. If you can spot him this time, you inform the commandant that you have recognized a notorious war criminal, high up on the list of US Army's black list. Then, that's where I come in, Colonel Ersenbrick. I take charge from then on in.'

Otto nodded glumly. This would be the fifth time he had been incarcerated in a special interrogation camp – and he didn't like it one bit. If it was not the lice and fleas, then it was the fellows pestering him in the seclusion of the latrines, 'Why, you are a handsome young fellow, Herr . . .' sort of thing, accompanied by the usual sickly smile and wandering hands. 'Christ,' he had exploded to Moishe more than once, 'you'd think on the hunger rations the English give them, their docks would have fallen off by this time, instead of thinking about a bit of the other!'

'Sex is eternal,' Moishe had answered with an easy shrug. 'Love triumphs over adversity, even in the pen.'

Otto's answer had not been one bit loving. Now it was going to happen all over again. While Moishe enjoyed the nubile charms of his latest 'frowlein' Trudi in Hamburg and the Count went about his good works (for he took his new role very seriously), he was going to have to spend another couple of days on black bread and *sirop*, washed down with that deadly English tea, fighting off the warm brothers[1] – and the lice. It was a hell of a way to enter the post-war world.

The commandant was a foppish young man with overlong hair and a thin black moustache, which looked as if he pencilled it on in front of the mirror every morning before he left his quarters. But in spite of his somewhat feminine appearance, he seemed to be very military in style and presentation. 'Regimental' was what he called it himself.

Standing at the window of his office, with the three cronies grouped politely around him, he pointed at the burly SS men striding back and forth, swinging their arms as if they were on parade, throwing up tremendous salutes in the English manner at imaginary officers, while others carried out the British army's slow march, mincing along like oversized ballet dancers with piles, and said: 'Trying to rehabilitate them, you see, Colonel Ersenbrick. Naturally they're baduns – and Huns, to boot. But drill, the good old British Army's square-bashing, will make soldiers of them yet. Before I'm finished with them, they'll have a lot of pride in the jolly old Number One Interrogation Camp. Regimental to their polished studs and full of the bash-on spirit,' he concluded enthusiastically, and slashed his cane against his side, as if he might enjoy a few whacks

[1] Homosexuals.

of the 'jolly old cane' (as he would undoubtedly have put it) now and again.

Inwardly, Otto groaned. He knew the type. These English public school people were the most outrageous perverts, and absolute yo-yos as well. Nobody, not even the English, could understand what made them tick.

'So as I see it, Colonel Ersenbrick, you are infiltrating Captain Stahl into my unit to do a little bit of . . . how should I put it . . . sneaking, what?' The camp commandant frowned. 'Not really cricket, what?'

Moishe knew his English. He had his answer ready. 'Rotten apples, Major! You want rid of your rotten apples. How can an outfit have unit pride, when there are rotten apples about?'

That did the trick. 'Of course, of course . . . never thought about it like that. Old Flashman at Rugby, messing up the good Doctor,' he said obscurely, 'that sort of thing.'

'Yes, that sort of thing,' Moishe agreed hastily, not having the faintest idea what the Englishman was talking about.

Outside the bemused prisoners were crying out in unison, as if they were British guardsmen, '*Up, two, three . . . down, two, three!*'

The chinless commandant beamed with pleasure. 'My God, do you hear that, gentlemen! Isn't it music to your ears? What perfection. Almost classic in its way!' He saw the sour look on Moishe's dark face and said, 'All right, Colonel, I'll organize Captain Stahl here.' He mustered Otto's uniform, with the dark patches across the breast where the medals and decorations had been, and the ripped off epaulettes. 'Looks all right to me,' he conceded. 'Yes, you look like the rest of them when they are brought in here. But, of course, we'll smarten you up in due course. Hm, yes, quite all right.' Suddenly he stared hard at Otto. 'Just one thing, Captain Stahl.'

'Yes?' Otto answered, suddenly apprehensive. 'What?'

'Well, as you know I am doing my very best to reform my chaps – drill and unit pride and all that – but unfortunately there are always some fellows who won't knuckle under. Odd men out and the like . . .'

'What are you trying to say, Major?'

'This. If these hard cases find out you're . . . er . . . a spy, something unpleasant might happen to you.'

The Count and Moishe looked worried. Otto swallowed hard and posed his question carefully. 'Like what, Major? What kind of unpleasantness, please?'

'Well, the last one we pulled out of the bogs. They'd drowned him in there.'

'You mean – *in the shithouse*?' Otto cried, aghast, his face suddenly ashen.

'Yes. Terrible mess they made of the place getting him out. Had to have the whole area whitewashed again. Spoiled the overall impression of the cam—'

'Did you hear that, Moishe?' Otto cried, drowning the Englishman's words. 'They croaked a spy in the shithouse! . . . *I'm not going!* Let me get out of here . . .'

Hastily, Moishe grabbed the abruptly panicked Otto by the arm and led him out of earshot. 'Listen, Otto,' he hissed urgently, while the commandant stared at the two of them in bewilderment, 'I'm never gonna be more than fifty yards away from you the whole of the time you spend in this dump. The Count and I will take it in turns, night and day. Never fear. Secondly you've got your pistol, if the worst comes to the worst.'

Otto opened his mouth to object.

Moishe didn't give him a chance. 'And thirdly, Otto, if you ever want to get on that green twig you're always going on about, this is the only way. If we're ever gonna get rich quick, old buddy, it's gonna be through Himmler.' He looked hard at the blond young German with dark cunning eyes. 'Think of the dough.'

Otto let his shoulders droop as if in defeat. 'All right,' he said, 'I'll do it . . .'

A few minutes later, after the Count, in his new role of the representative of the Swedish Red Cross, had handed out a few tins of sardines to the clamouring prisoners, Otto was placed in the care of an enormous red-faced sergeant-major, whose eyes were hidden by the visor of his peaked cap so that he looked as if he were eyeless. But his voice was still very much in evidence. Lowering his mouth so that it was level with Otto's right ear, he bellowed at full blast, as if he were still on the square at the depot of the Brigade of Guards, 'All right, you 'orrible little man! At the double! *MOVE IT!*'

Miserably Otto Stahl moved it. Otto was behind barbed wire, a prisoner-of-war yet again[1].

For the next twenty-four hours a very worried Otto Stahl checked the camp out, making sure he avoided the English drill-sergeants, who were always hustling groups of reluctant prisoners into drill squads to march them up and down the dusty square, throwing quivering salutes to left and right. As was always the case in such camps, the prisoners, he knew from experience, could be divided into the 'hearties', the ones who still tried to keep fit, stripping off their shirts at first ray of sunshine – 'Vitamin C, you know' – eating dandelion leaves raw – 'bursting with vitamins and minerals' – even indulging in physical jerks, in spite of the starvation rations the Tommies fed them. Then there were 'funnies', who engaged in a myriad strange activities from playing home-made flutes in the solitude of the stinking latrines to attempting to distil potato-schnaps from carefully hoarded potato peelings. But it was the 'loners' who mainly interested Otto: those cut-off, introverted individuals who walked round and round the camp circuit by themselves, mumbling under their breath; or who stood staring at the wire for hours on end, as if they could see something beyond it known only to them; or who holed themselves up in the wooden barracks, blankets pulled over their heads, as if to cut out the daylight, shaking and trembling like frozen puppies.

Otto reasoned that if Himmler were in this particular camp, he would attempt to avoid the company of his fellows. Among the higher ranking SS officers, there would

[1] See *Otto and the Tommies* for further details.

be some who might well have met him at one time or another; and Himmler would have realized by now, even his black guards might betray him to the Tommies for a tin of corned beef and a packet of Woodbines. In this new defeated Germany, honour had been tossed overboard swiftly. Now hunger, and the best way to satisfy it, was the only thing that counted.

As always, he discovered there were the usual weird 'loners' in the camp. There was 'Adolf' for instance, reputed to be a former *gauleiter*, who did realistic imitations of the Führer for the benefit of the Tommies, including a spectacular carpet-biting imitation of Hitler in a rage, rolling around the compound in the dust, snapping at the earth like a rabid dog. This usually earned him a round of admiring applause from the guards and a shower of cigarettes. There was the 'Spirit of the Third Reich', as he proclaimed himself, an elderly 'golden pheasant', who walked with a Groucho Marx lope, who wore make-up, whitening his face with chalk and darkening the bags beneath his sad eyes with a blue-bag, and would sit for hours in front of the main entrance to the camp, arms folded like a Red Indian across his chest, reciting long passages from *Mein Kampf* to the bemused sentries. There were no cigarettes for his performance, and Otto had a suspicion that the 'golden pheasant' would have disdained them, even if they had been offered. He was really weird. Yet Himmler, if he were really hidden somewhere in the big sprawling POW cage, obstinately refused to surface.

Otto began to despair. He would never land on that fabled 'green twig'.

FOUR

It was on the second night of Otto's incarceration that he finally struck lucky. He had wandered morosely over to the recreation hut, for want of something better to do, and had planted himself on one of the wooden benches at the far end of the place, which was heavy with stink of boiled cabbage (their evening meal) and the sickly odour of home-made cigarettes, fashioned out of latrine paper and tea-leaves, to find himself in the midst of the camp's amateur dramatic society's rehearsals. The society, Otto learned later, had been the brain-child of the camp commandant who, as he told Moishe with a strange smirk on his chinless face, had 'always been fond of a little bit of harmless dressing up'.

'Yer, as the shitting fairy queen, I'll be bound!' Otto had snorted indignantly afterwards when Moishe had reported the conversation with the English major. 'That Tommy is as funny as a fruit-cake!'

There was the usual crowd of prisoners who favoured that kind of thing around, crowding onto the improvised stage, all waving hands and limp wrists, over-rouged and absurd in their too tight, too short skirts, made out of blackout curtains, tugging at their suspenders as they bent over to reveal bottoms, deliberately clothed in the same black material.

It was the kind of heated mutual-admiration society that he had seen often enough in the camps, a mixture of blatant sexuality and male shame that both amused and appalled him. Indeed, looking at them now, as they were formed up into a rough-and-ready chorus line by a slim young officer with plucked eyebrows, wearing a dress made from latrine sacking (though the general impression was spoilt by the fact he was smoking a pipe and his feet were clad in battered jackboots) he felt a little sad for them.

Why did men without women get themselves into such a mess? Why indeed? He sucked his teeth glumly and watched.

'Now then, girls,' the young blond officer with the plucked eyebrows lisped, rolling his eye coquettishly, 'I wish you would get into position . . .'

Somebody simpered under his breath and the others laughed in a silver girlish way.

'Not *that* position, darling,' the blond officer said and waved a limp-wristed hand at the culprit. 'I do declare, Heinz, that's all you've got on your mind.'

The man in question clutched his genitals and gave a mock, high-pitched scream, 'Oh, you naughty girl, you know very well that it's not in my head that I've got *it*!' He rolled his made-up eyes significantly, and the others tittered yet again.

Otto felt a little sick. He half-rose and was preparing to go when no less a person than the camp commandant himself strolled in and, with a cheerful wave of his absurd cane, cried at the chorus line, already beginning to stiffen into the position of attention, 'No bull, chaps. Just a social visit. Please *do* carry on.' And with that, he removed his cap, touched his moustache, as if to satisfy himself that it was still there, and sat down, eyes suddenly glinting as he fixed his gaze on the blond officer with the pipe. Otto nodded his head significantly; so *that* was it!

'*Also, los!*' the blond officer with the plucked eyebrows commanded. '*Das lied – jetzt!*'

The man at the battered piano struck up the first chords and the clumsy chorus sprang into action, advancing towards the centre of the stage in a ragged line, ogling the non-existent audience in a pathetic parody of female seductiveness, raising first their right legs and then their left to show their crude knickers and at the same time gasping some sort of a song in a language which Otto at first did not understand. Was it supposed to be French, he asked himself? For those miserable imitations in front of him, French would appear to be the language of love.

Then he caught a word he recognized – and another –

and in the same instant as he realized they were singing in English, the whole mob of them turned, bent, thrust out their black-clad bottoms, wriggling them in what they presumably thought was a sexy manner, and bellowed as one, '*Right in the Führer's face!*'

Up front, the camp commandant clapped his hands in sheer delight and declared in a loud voice, 'Oh, I say, jolly good. *Right in the Führer's face!* How delightfully vulgar!'

The red-faced chorus beamed at him in respectful pleasure, one or two of them heaving their artificial bosoms back into place; while the blond officer in the frock pursed his lips and came forward slowly and languorously, swaying his hips seductively, giving the camp commandant a significant look from beneath his plucked eyebrows à la Marlene Dietrich at her siren-like best.

Otto cursed. He felt sick and disgusted. How low could his fellow Germans sink in order to toady to their new bosses? Fancy picking up that coarse American song of 1943, with its vulgar chorus, as a means of integrating themselves with the Tommies. It was goddam nauseating. He grabbed his cap and thrust back his bench with an angry oath. 'Brown-nosers,' he called to the men on the stage. 'You ought to get yer army numbers printed on the soles of yer boots so that decent folk'll know who yer were. Getting up the Tommies' arses so deep like that!'

There were cries of protest from the dancers and the blond officer simpered, 'Oh you're only jealous, whoever you are. Don't take one bit of notice of him, girls.' He giggled a little hysterically. 'You see he's just had an unhappy love-affair. He broke his right hand!'

He made an explicit obscene gesture with his clenched fist and the chorus broke out into wild laughter, while the camp commandant blushed and said, 'I say, Klaus, that's going a little too far, you know. That's the sort of thing that a chap does in the privacy of his own quarters.'

'Oh, stick yer salami up yer own ass and give yersen a cheap thrill,' a red-faced Otto flung angrily over his shoulder and blundered, eyes burning, out of the recreation hut. In his rage, he nearly knocked over the skinny little man with the black patch over one eye, who had apparently been scouring the naked earth in front of the hut in the hope that the camp commandant might have thrown away a cigarette end before he entered.

Otto caught him just in time and prevented him from falling. 'Watch it now . . .' He stopped short.

The sallow-faced man straightened up, a smile on his thin lips. 'I heard what you did inside there, sir. May I humbly beg leave to congratulate you on your loyalty to our poor dead Führer.'

Otto's heart skipped a beat. It had to be him.

The man with the eye-patch, wearing the shabby grey uniform of a policeman in the defeated Greater German Wehrmacht snapped sloppily to attention and barked in his thin voice, 'Sergeant Hitzinger of the former Field Security Police reporting, sir!'

'At ease . . . at ease, Sergeant,' Otto heard himself say, as if he were speaking from a million kilometres away. There was no mistaking the man standing to attention in front of him. It was *him*; it was *Reichsführer* SS Heinrich 'Harrykins' Himmler! He'd found him at last. Otto could have jumped high into the air with joy . . .

'Rats, Captain Stahl!' Himmler cried bitterly, as they strolled away from the hut towards the wire. From inside came the strains of the chorus singing now, 'Roll out ze barrel . . . Ze gang's all here . . . Ve're going to have a bagful of fon . . .'

'Rats abandoning the sinking ship.' Himmler's jowls shook angrily and his sallow face flushed.

He threw a bitter look at 'Adolf', who was grovelling in the dust for the benefit of the Tommies once again, crying in guttural English, 'Peace, I only vant *peace* . . . A *piece* of Austria, a *piece* of Poland . . . a *piece* of everyding . . .'

'They will do anything for cigarettes . . . Traitors to a man. That our beloved Führer should have been fated to have led such a rabble . . .' Himmler shook his head bitterly and could say no more, his one hand in his pocket, counting the treasured cigarette ends he had picked up that afternoon.

'Not all, Sergeant,' Otto said grandly, playing the arrogant SS officer bit to the full. 'Not all of us have surrendered to the Anglo-Saxons . . .' he touched his chest '. . . in here, at least.'

Himmler paused a moment and stared up at Otto's hard Aryan face in admiration, which turned an instant later into bewilderment. 'But where, if a humble sergeant is allowed to ask, Captain, is your armband?' He pointed at the lighter patch on Otto's right sleeve.

It was precisely the opening that Otto had been waiting for. He stopped too, and looked carefully to right and left, as if he wanted to be sure that no one else was listening. 'Sergeant, once I belonged to the *Leibstandarte*, the concrete-crushers, as they used to call us[1]. Ha, ha,' he gave what he hoped was a tough SS officer's laugh. 'But after my fifth wound in Russia I was transferred to – the *SD*[2].' He closed one eye deliberately and tapped the right side of his nose in the German fashion. 'Wooden eye be careful, *was*?'

'Exactly, exactly, my dear Captain Stahl.' Himmler gave a cold little smile. 'I see in here we all have our – er – little secrets.'

Otto looked down at the *Reichsführer* frostily. 'Sergeant,' he barked, 'we of the SS have only one secret. The knowledge of how to die bravely for our beloved Germany!'

Himmler pressed his knees together in ecstasy like a little boy who wants to urinate in a hurry. 'Well, well said, Captain,' he breathed fervently. 'My God, when the whole world collapses, the SS continues to fight.' Himmler's eyes flooded with tears. 'What stout fellows you are! Spirit completely unbroken!'

Otto felt an absolute fool, but he had just spotted the camp commandant leaving the hut, arm in arm with the officer with the plucked eyebrows. It was an apt moment

[1] The *Leibstandarte*, Hitler's Bodyguard, was nicknamed the 'concrete crushers' because of the many parades it gave in Berlin before the war.
[2] The SS's own secret service.

for a demonstration of his 'unbroken spirit'. He stamped to attention and, thrusting out his chin defiantly, started to bellow the bold words of the 'Horst Wessel' song, at the top of his voice.

At the Englishman's side, the officer with the plucked eyebrows flinched as if someone had struck him a physical blow. What was the big fool singing that terrible Nazi marching song now for? But the camp commandant took it in his stride. 'Always know when a unit has got spirit, Klaus,' he declared and squeezed his companion's arm with delight. 'The chaps sing. Yessir, they sing!' He raised his absurd little cane and cried, 'Good show! Carry on singing, that man!' Then he went on his way, his mind racing excitedly, as his new-found friend told of the delightful things they were going to do together.

Otto spat contemptuously into the dust. 'English pig-dog,' he grunted, his defiant song finished. 'The whole damned decadent pack of them are interested in piggeries such as that!'

Himmler gazed up at Otto, his short-sighted eye full of admiration. 'The wonderful spirit of the SS, Captain. Not even the cage and its hardships can break it.' Suddenly he spotted an abandoned cigarette-end and just prevented himself in time from bending to pick it up. Besides, one of the crueller Tommies had ground it deliberately under his heel anyway.

Otto shrugged his shoulders carelessly. 'What is there to fear, Sergeant, save death itself? Come on, let us walk.'

Himmler hesitated a moment. The cigarette-end stared up at him temptingly. He forced himself to be as hard as the young man at his side. 'Sir, young sir,' he declared, 'if our beloved Führer had only possessed another thousand SS officers like you, we would not have lost this war so cruelly.'

'Fuck that for a tale!' Otto sneered to himself. Aloud he said, 'Who knows, Sergeant, who knows? One day our beloved Germany will rise again and march once more – to defy and shock the whole world!'

Himmler shook visibly, as if he might fall into a swoon

at any moment. 'Do you really think so, Captain Stahl . . . Please tell me, do you really think so?'

'I do not *think* so, I *know* so!' Otto barked harshly, telling himself that the old fart was going to have an orgasm in half a minute the way he looked. 'Come now, let us walk.'

Himmler grabbed his arm. 'Please . . . please, let me be your friend, Captain Stahl. I beg you . . .'

Outside a blurred voice was singing, '*Drunk last night, drunk the night before, gonna get drunk tonight like I've never been bleedin' drunk before . . .*'

Otto told himself, desperately fighting back his revulsion at the proximity of this miserable monster, that he wished at that moment he could get 'bleedin' drunk' too. The man made him sick. 'Yes, yes,' he said thickly, vomit already flooding his throat, even as he spoke, 'you can be my friend Sergeant Hitzinger.'

Heinrich Himmler hugged Otto's arm in sheer delight.

Otto retched.

FIVE

'Leo, I thought I'd pulled it off at last . . . I was heading straight for that green twig, that you accuse me of always rabbiting on about . . . I had the Reichsheini – that's the nickname we gave him in those days – in the palm of my shitting big hand!'

Even now, two years later, I can still see Otto clenching his fingers together as if he were squeezing the throat of the long dead Herr Himmler, his ancient wrinkled face contorted with rage, as he sat there on the balcony of his villa, staring out at the even green of the Med.

'I was quids in with him. Himmler, I mean. I had him almost eating out of my hand. You see, Otto, he needed a friend like I need a right arm. The last few weeks had knocked all the piss and vinegar out of him. He was a nobody, a one-eyed sergeant of a defeated army, surrounded by officers, many of whom had belonged to his own frigging SS and would have sold their arseholes for a packet of them Golden Flak cigarettes, or what ever those Tommy lung torpedoes of them days were called.'

'Gold Flake,' I had corrected him gently, wondering at his rage at events which had taken place over forty years before. 'But what happened, Otto?'

'*Nothing fuckin' well happened!*' he had snorted bitterly. 'That was the trouble. Here I was, with Himmler now my best friend – in a pig's arse! – ready to spill his guts, tell me where the loot was hidden. Christ on a crutch, I was like a sixteen-year-old virgin panting to get my first taste of the old salami between her legs –'

'*What happened*, Otto?' I had repeated firmly, because once Otto gets started nothing will stop him. He has that unfortunate German tendency to verbal diarrhoea. '*Please!*'

He had taken a deep breath and, his eyes still bitter at the memory of what had happened that dark day at umber One Interrogation Camp in that fateful summer of 1945, he had plunged into his sad story . . .

'You see, Captain Stahl,' Himmler was saying, 'I, like you, have a little secret . . .' Himmler looked anxiously to left and right, but the other occupants of his hut were either asleep in their bunks already or grouped at the rough plank table, chatting in a desultory fashion or playing *skat* without enthusiasm. 'I am not what I seem to be,' he concluded with a tight, cold smile.

Otto's heart raced and his nerves tingled electrically, but his face showed nothing of his emotional turmoil. It remained haughty and arrogant, as befitted that of a much decorated SS officer listening to the ramblings of a lowly police sergeant. 'Yes, and who are you then, Sergeant?' he forced himself to ask in a bored, uninterested manner.

Himmler licked his lips. 'Prepare for a shock, young friend,' he said hoarsely.

Otto tensed and prepared for Himmler's final revelation. But the expected shock came from elsewhere.

Suddenly there was a thunderous hammering on the door. 'Outside, outside!' a harsh beery voice yelled in English. '*Spot check . . . Outside everybody . . . Raus . . . raus . . . Appell . . . Outside!*'

Abruptly all was confusion, as whistles shrilled urgently and the Tommies beat on the doors of the huts with their pickaxe handles, bellowing at the tops of their voices; while the startled prisoners hurriedly hid whatever they thought should be hidden from prying eyes, before stumbling to the doors and out into the square.

Otto was forced out with the rest, Himmler hanging onto him like a frightened child might do to its mother, crying urgently above the racket, 'Not a word of my secret, Stahl, I beg you . . . It is a matter of life and death . . . Not a word . . .'

Outside, the guards were already forming the prisoners up in long lines, while a worried camp commandant looked on, slapping his cane anxiously, or so Otto thought, against his right leg Next to him stood a group of strange officers, who, Otto told himself, had cop written all over them. They stared at the startled prisoners forming up in front of them with that typical tough stony look of the bull – full of the arrogant knowledge that they were on the winning side and always would be. Bulls could make a criminal of anyone, innocent or not; it was one of the perks of their job. Otto felt a cold finger of fear trace its way down his own spine, as a trembling Himmler clutched his hand. The big eyeless sergeant-major stamped up to the waiting officers and bellowed at the top of his voice in his usual fashion, 'Parade, all present and correct, *sir*! . . . Parade ready for inspection, *sir*!' He swung the chinless wonder a tremendous salute, his hand trembling at the peak of his cap, as if he were in the throes of some tropical fever.

'Thank you, Sarnt-Major.' The camp commandant turned to the strange officers. 'Gentlemen,' he announced, 'they're all yours.'

The smaller of the three officers, a dark-faced man with a trim military moustache and hard black eyes, grunted something, then, followed by the other two, started to walk the length of the first rank, stopping and staring hard at each fearful German face, as if he were trying to impress the features onto his mind's eye for ever.

Otto gulped. He could guess what the surprise parade was for, especially as the two other officers held big books in their hands, which they consulted every now and again in response to a question from their leader. They were security cops. They were searching for what the Tommies called 'war criminals'.

An ashen-faced Himmler must have come to the same conclusion, too, for he hissed out of the side of his mouth, as if he were some old jailbird, who had spent years behind the 'Swedish curtains'[1], 'Not a word of what I said, Stahl, not a word!'

'Shut yer face!' the officer with the plucked eyebrows who was standing to the other side of the shaking *Reichsführer* whispered urgently. 'We don't want any attention

[1] German slang for prison-bars.

drawn to us.' There was a sudden rushing noise and Otto stared down curiously, in spite of his fear, thinking the pansified officer might well have suffered an unfortunate accident. But that wasn't the case. Sand, not urine, was trickling down the inside of his right leg onto the ground. The stupid sod had been caught by the snap check right in the middle of emptying the sand from a tunnel. He was an escaper! Otto could have moaned out loud.

Slowly the English bulls came ever closer to where Himmler stood trembling visibly, and with the sudden, total recognition of a vision, Otto knew the one-eyed fool would spill his guts. 'Hold on,' he hissed urgently. 'Hold on, for God's sake!'

'I can't, Herr Stahl,' Himmler replied miserably, misunderstanding Otto's command. 'I have a terribly weak bladder. It's trickling down my right leg already.'

Otto gave a low moan and gave in. He let it happen. And it did. The little officer stopped in front of Himmler, whom he would later describe in his official report when the tragedy was all over as 'small, ill-looking and shabbily dressed'. He had decided to leave out the bit about the suspicious stain on his right leg; Monty was a bit of a prude. He gave Himmler a long, hard look. He took his time in the way of all cops, believing as they always did that a man was guilty until he was proved innocent. Finally he broke the heavy brooding silence and asked in flawless German, 'What is your name and rank?'

Himmler licked suddenly parched lips. Otto tensed. Was he going to spill his guts? He pressed his nails into the palms of his hands cruelly, willing the stupid shit not to talk.

'Sergeant Hitz –' Himmler began and then his nerve finally broke. In one and the same movement, he removed his eye-patch and put on that schoolmaster's pince-nez that was known throughout the world. 'Himmler, Heinrich,' he said in a soft almost inaudible voice and held out his hands, as if for the handcuffs.

Up front, the camp commandant gave a soft moan and

fainted. At that moment, Otto would have gladly fainted, too, and blotted this whole mess out for damn good.

Otto never learned till long after the war what had happened to his new friend that day, as the parade dissolved in uproar, with Himmler being frog-marched away by a group of brawny NCOs to the boos and cheers of his former SS elite. In the end the last hours of the *Reichsführer* SS became a tragi-comedy. Stripped to his underpants and wrapped in a grey army blanket he was brought before a doctor and Colonel Ewart, Montgomery's Chief of Intelligence, and once again confronted with the fact that he was indeed Heinrich Himmler, to which he now replied he wasn't. It had all been a terrible mistake.

The English guessed that Himmler was playing for time, but to what purpose they couldn't guess – and, of course, they never found out. Otto's own guess, long after the event, was that 'Natch, he was going to offer them a substantial share of the loot if they'd get him away from Germany. It was all part of the cunning bugger's plan – he knew the Tommies were the only ones who could smuggle him out of the country. There was no relying on the Germans any more.' But then that was typical Otto. He always sees things in terms of dollars and cents.

At all events, Ewart ordered the MO to examine the *Reichsführer* once more. Sergeant-Major Austin of the Pioneer Corps, who was guarding Himmler, had already found L-Pills (L for 'lethal', naturally) in the German's clothing and Ewart was taking no chances.

Reluctantly Doctor Wells, the medical officer in question, began to re-examine Himmler in the tight little office. Finally he reached Himmler's mouth, full of bad teeth and gold fillings. Wells frowned. 'You'd better have a dentist look at those molars,' he grunted. 'They don't look too healthy to me.'

'Come off it, Doc,' Ewart snapped. 'He'll be swinging at the end of a rope, I'll be bound, before this year is out.

Bugger his teeth –' he stopped short and bent forward suddenly. 'What's that black knob back there, Doc?'

'What black knob . . . the light in here is terrible.'

Dr Wells pushed a struggling Himmler closer to the poor light shed by the single, naked electric bulb. 'Quick Sarnt-Major,' he barked at Austin, 'give me a hand!'

'Sir!' Austin added all the muscle he had built up over years of heaving trash into the corporation muck-cart to the efforts of the doctor and Colonel Ewart to push a wriggling and writhing Himmler to the light.

Finally they had the *Reichsführer* in position. Now he stubbornly refused to open his mouth. But Sergeant-Major Austin was up to the situation. 'Get ready, sir!' he yelled and pinched Himmler's nose very hard.

Himmler yelled with pain and Wells thrust his two front fingers inside his mouth. But he had not anticipated that Himmler would react so quickly. He bit down hard.

'Ouch,' Wells cried, 'the bugger's gone and bit me!'

For one last moment, Himmler looked from face to face: Austin's bluff working-man's features; Wells, the doctor's, flushed and angry; Ewart's worn and worried. He made his decision. With all his strength he bit down hard. The L-Pill burst. He felt it crunch on his tongue, releasing the deadly poison immediately. He swallowed deliberately, knowing that by doing so he was condemning himself to death, a cold smile on his flushed face. 'I shall be remembered for a thousand years,' he began. Suddenly his face contorted with absolute, unbearable agony, as the poison exploded with fury inside him, tearing and ripping at his innards in red-hot burning, searing pain. His knees started to buckle beneath him.

'Grab him, Austin!' Wells yelled in alarm, fastening his hands around the dying man's throat, strangling him in an attempt to prevent the poison entering his body.

Ewart flung open the door. The camp commandant stood there, trembling like a newly-born puppy. 'Needle and thread! . . . at the double!' he barked.

'Needle and thread?' the major quavered hopelessly.

'Get it from me housewife, sir!' the eyeless sergeant-major reacted immediately. He sprang to the nearest desk and, pulling out his 'housewife', the soldier's issue sewing-kit, threaded the needle with amazing speed for someone who appeared to have no eyes.

Ewart grabbed it. 'Open his mouth, Austin!' he cried.

Next instant he had pierced the unconscious man's purple tongue with the needle, drawn the cotton through it and forced it out of Himmler's mouth like a piece of wet leather. Wells thrust home the tube of the stomach pump. Now all three of them sweated, their faces glazed as if with vaseline, while Wells worked on the German, using the rubber instruments, while at the same time administering emetics.

But *Reichsführer* Himmler was failing fast. Wells dropped the pump. 'Get him on the floor,' he cried urgently. 'Quick now, we're going to lose him otherwise!'

Swiftly they lowered Himmler to the floor. Wells sprang on top of him. In those days the 'kiss-of-life' had not yet been invented. If it had, Heinrich Himmler's last experience of this world would have been that of being kissed by an unshaven British army doctor. Instead, Wells worked his arms back and forth furiously, slamming his clenched fist down on Himmler's heart at regular intervals.

To no avail! Himmler was failing very fast. Sweating and gasping for breath, Wells ceased his labours and felt for Himmler's pulse, while the other two stared down at them helplessly. Slowly, very slowly, he shook his head and said, 'He's had it.'

'Blast!' Ewart cried.

'Bugger it!' Austin agreed in his more working-class manner.

Almost sadly, Wells closed the *Reichsführer*'s eyes for the last time, while Austin went to fetch another blanket; the other was wet with Himmler's urine. Carelessly he draped it over the face of the one-time most feared man in Europe. For a moment the three of them simply stood there, without any feeling of reverence for the dead, the doctor's chest heaving, as if he had just run a great race, drained of any kind of feeling. Finally Colonel Ewart said tonelessly, as if he were speaking about a hunk of diseased meat, 'Get rid of him Sarnt-Major . . . See that nobody knows where you bury him. We don't want to start any bloody legends . . . or have the Jerries digging him up in years to come.' He stared glumly at the blanket-draped corpse. 'My God, I wouldn't like to have his conscience, wherever the bugger might be now.'

'In hell!' Austin said and then remembered with whom he was talking and added a hasty 'sir'. The other two did not even notice . . .

It is recorded that Sergeant-Major Austin wrapped the body of the ex-chicken farmer who had ravaged half of Europe in an army grey blanket. This he covered with a camouflage net, which he secured with some telephone wire scrounged from the Corps of Signals. Alone, and taking great care that no one followed him, he set off for the woods with Himmler over one shoulder and a shovel on the other. By dead of night, with the only sound the hooting of the wood owls and his own harsh laboured breathing, he buried the *Reichsführer* SS Heinrich Himmler. It somehow seemed fitting that the leader of those feared black guards, with the dread skull-and-cross-bones insignia on their caps, should have been buried by a man who, in another life, had been an employee of his local town council, working in the humble but highly useful capacity of local refuse disposal. A dustman, in other words . . .

SIX

Otto slept fitfully, tossing and turning in the narrow wooden bunk, snoring at times and then relapsing into what sounded more like a moan of pain.

As soon as they had taken Himmler away, he had tried to get into the administrative wing of the camp, fighting his way through the angry, shouting POWs who besieged the place, shaking their fists and crying, '*Release him . . . release the Reichsführer!*'

But it had been no use. Armed Tommy guards swarmed everywhere, their faces hard and set, their fingers curled round the triggers of their rifles, as if they were itching to open fire at these damned impertinent Germans, who still didn't know that they were defeated. In the end he had given up. It was safer that way, he concluded. He would sneak into the offices next morning after first parade and let the camp commandant have him smuggled out. There was nothing more he could do here. Himmler was gone and with him all knowledge of where that damned loot might be.

Now Otto was dreaming. He was climbing a mountain of gold coins, each one as big as rock and just as slippery. Time and time again he tried to ascend in an attempt to grasp the bright green twig which flourished so tantalizingly at the top of this mountain of gold; and time and time again he slipped and went slithering and sliding painfully down to the bottom once more, where a crowd of burly SS thugs armed with clubs and dressed in black knickers and fish-net stockings kicked and thumped him. All the while Himmler looked on, jumping up and down and clapping his pudgy little hands with joy, every time that Otto came tumbling down once more, crying in a shrill voice, 'You'll never make that green twig, Otto, my dear . . . you never will . . .'

'Open yer peepers, yer treacherous bastard . . . Come on now, open those shitting glassy orbs!' The harsh, menacing hiss seemed to come from a long, long way away. But there was no mistaking the hate and the venom in the voice. A fist thudded painfully into his side and Otto awoke with a start as that mountain of gold vanished for good.

He shook his head. It felt twice its normal size. Slowly the mist in front of his eyes began to drift away. He looked through narrowed eyes at his hand. It was covered with blood. Something – someone – had injured his head. Gradually his eyes focused. He could make out shadowy shapes, seen as if through a mist, closing in all around him. He blinked several times, quickly, as if he could not quite believe the evidence of his own eyes.

Now he saw them, the wolfish, rapacious faces of his fellow-prisoners staring down at him as he lay there, hollowed out to death's-heads by the wavering light of a solitary candle held by the blond officer with the plucked eyebrows.

'Bastard, are you awake at last?' With his free hand the officer slapped Otto's face – hard.

'Hey, what –' Otto began in sudden rage. A heavy hand pressed down on his mouth and cut off his cry of protest almost immediately.

'We do the talking here, rat!' the blond officer snapped from his thin-lipped, savage mouth. He nodded to the giant holding Otto's mouth. 'All right, let him go. We don't want to kill him – *just yet*!' he sneered. 'But if he opens his trap to make the slightest sound, croak him!'

'With the greatest of pleasure,' the giant answered and lifted up his paw slowly.

Otto sucked in a great gasp of air and stared around at the hard, bitter emaciated faces in sudden fear. There was death written on each and every one of them.

'Right,' the blond officer snapped. 'I am going to give you the right to defend yourself.'

'*Defend* –' Otto's question ended in a yelp of pain, as the blond officer slapped him.

'I'm doing the talking here, remember.'

Otto nodded carefully, feeling the hot, wet blood begin to trickle down from his right nostril, telling himself he was in bad trouble, very bad trouble.

'So you betrayed the *Reichsführer* to those Tommy bastards,' the blond officer continued in his harsh brutal manner, which marked him, too, as an ex-SS officer. 'Why? For cigarettes? To ingratiate yourself with the enemy? Or,' he paused significantly, and Otto sensed the others holding their breath, as if they already half-knew what was to come, 'are you something else?' he hissed. '*Speak*.'

'I didn't betray Himmler!' Otto said desperately. 'And I'm just like you . . . a simple prisoner-of-war the Tommies picked up for questioning and slung into this damned place.' He looked from one hard face to the other, but they remained stony in their disbelief.

'Is that so?' The blond officer held up his middle finger. It was smudged with what looked like indelible ink. 'Just like us,' he sneered, 'a simple POW, eh? Well, how come the SS blood group under your arm, supposedly *tattooed* on when you entered our formation, came off so easily, as if it had been printed on the day before yesterday? How do you explain that – *simple prisoner-of-war*?'

'Yes, yes,' the others growled. 'Explain that . . . where did you get that mark from?' They pressed ever closer, their faces angry, eyes gleaming with rage, and looking to Otto, now scared out of his wits, highly dangerous.

Otto could have cursed out loud, at the Americans' and his own stupidity at believing their 'expert' who had set him and the Count up for their mission to Wewelsberg. What had he said? 'No sweat, Otto. This is *better* than the real thing.' Now this blond fiend had simply wet his pinkie and rubbed off the SS blood group, just like that. 'Please,' he cried desperately over the mounting noise, 'please, let me explain . . .'

'There will be no explanations, rat!' the blond officer rasped, eyes burning into Otto. 'You have been tried and sentenced!'

'Tried and sentenced?'

'Yes,' the officer yelled, '*sentenced to death*!'

'To the crapper with him!' the cry went up on all sides. '*To the crapper with the traitor!*'

Otto could have pissed himself there and then. They were going to do to him what they had done to other traitors. They were going to drown him in the shit of the big thunderboxes. '*No!*' he screamed, '*no, please!*' He tried to get away, but he didn't stand a chance. Suddenly they were all over him, slamming his body with their fists, spitting in his face, ripping at his hair like angry schoolgirls, and in an instant he was thrust into the air, scores of hands heaving him upwards. A door was kicked open. He could feel the cold draught. And then they were carrying him . . . *carrying him to the crappers* . . .

Moishe MacTavish slammed the door open. Behind him the Count, panting as if he had just run a race, blundered into his back, as the little American came to an abrupt halt.

In the centre of the camp office, the commandant was bent over his desk sobbing, as if heartbroken, while the eyeless sergeant-major, still wearing his guardsman's cap, was patting his shoulder, tendering him a cup of tea and saying softly, 'Try to get this down you, sir. I've put a drop of Nelson's blood in it. It'll do yer good, sir, you'll see.'

'But I couldn't touch a thing, Sarnt-Major,' the camp commandant wept, the black crayon which he used to colour his moustache every morning dripping down his sloping chin on to his blotter, like black tears. 'Oh, the shame of it! The shame . . . To think that I harboured such a swine . . . like that Himmler . . . in my camp. My God, he could have corrupted all my chaps, just when I had got them started so nicely on close order drill!' He started to sob once more, shoulders heaving wildly.

'Now, now, sir . . . Don't take on so,' the NCO tried to pacify him. 'They was doing beautiful on the slow march this morning . . . I'll get 'em onto the general salute – for you *personally* tomorrow, sir. You'll see. It'll be a real treat.'

Moishe exploded with rage. With a vicious swipe, he knocked the tea out of the big NCO's hand. 'Stick yer general salute up ya keester!' he yelled, beside himself with rage and fear. 'Don't you know what's going on in there?'

'Now steady on, *sir*,' the big NCO growled, doubling a right fist like a small steam shovel. 'This ain't the American army, you know, *sir*. All Coca-Cola and them sticky chocolate bars, *sir*. This is the British Kate Karney, *sir*.' He emphasized that 'sir' yet again, his voice full of menace.

Moishe got the message. The big Limey looked as if he could pull a fellow's right leg off easily – and beat him to death with it, without even breathing hard. He restrained himself with difficulty. 'Sorry, sorry, for coming in like this,' he said urgently. 'But we've still got our guy in there and we haven't heard from him since they took away Himmler. Can't you imagine that all hell is being let loose in there at this moment. Christ on a crutch,' he added wildly, his heart thumping frantically, 'anything – *everything* – could be happening to Captain Stahl.'

The camp commandant looked up at him, his chinless face tragic in its grief. 'Do you mean to say that there . . . are cases of indiscipline in *my camp*?' he asked in a broken voice.

'From the racket I just heard,' Moishe retorted hotly, 'they're tearing the frigging place apart!'

'Oh, my God!' It was too much for the camp commandant. 'After all that drill.' The right side of his face quivered frantically and he started to cry again.

Absently the eyeless NCO patted him on the shoulder, but with his attention now concentrated on the flushed little American. 'Did I hear you correct, like, sir,' he asked in that ponderous manner of his, 'when you said there was some sort of racket going on inside the perimeter, like?'

'Yes, yes!' the Count cried urgently, catching his breath again at last. 'I could hear them yelling "kill . . . kill" in German. Oh, you must hurry. Herr Stahl's life might well be in danger!'

The big noncom took his time, as befitted a senior non-commissioned officer. He adjusted his webbing belt, picked up his brass-shod pacing stick, stuck it formally under his right arm, and stamped down his foot with such energy that the whole room seemed to vibrate. He swung the weeping camp commandant a tremendous salute and bellowed in a roar that made Moishe wince with pain, 'Permission to withdraw, *sir*?'

The camp commandant did not look up. Instead he waved a soaked white lace handkerchief in the NCO's general direction.

'Thank you, sir!'

Stiffly, as if he were on parade, followed by the two comrades, he stalked to the door, leaving the camp commandant saying miserably to himself, 'One rotten apple. That's all it takes . . . Just one rotten apple . . .'

'*NO!*' Otto screamed . . . '*PLEASE, NO!*' His face contorted with the absolute horror of this terrible thing which was happening to *him*, Otto fought in panic-stricken fury to free himself from the hands which gripped him.

In front of him in the stinking half-darkness of the big communal latrine, the other prisoners-of-war grunted and tugged under the direction of the grim-faced blond officer, as they attempted to raise the lid of the privy. 'Once again,' he commanded. 'Heave – and up!'

This time they succeeded. Otto's nostrils were assailed by the sickening, cloying stench of human waste. He stared horror-stricken, as the jeering, shouting mob forced him ever closer. A mass of heaving yellow ordure confronted him, the rats that lived off it scuttling away into the darkness, startled by these sudden intruders. '*You can't*,' he screamed piteously. '*You can't* . . .'

'Can't we!' the blond officer yelled. 'Grab him up, comrades!'

Otto dodged. An officer tried to stop him. Otto's fist lashed out. He went reeling back, spitting out teeth, glittering like polished ivory in the blood-red mess of his mouth. 'He's getting away!' they screamed in fury. '*Los*, grab him, comrades!'

Desperate, the adrenalin pumping energy into his bloodstream, Otto evaded another pair of hands. To his left was the hessian screen which protected the latrine from public view. He headed for it, the pack after him. An officer dived at his flying heels. Otto lashed out instinctively. The officer howled in pain and fell beside the dripping slippery duckboards. Otto exerted the last of his strength, heart pumping all-out. The hessian loomed up. He took a deep breath and slammed into it.

It held!

Next moment he was down on his knees and they were hammering him with their fists, belabouring his ribs with their boots, crying and cursing him, some of them so carried away with anger that they were undoing their flies, as if they wished to urinate on this traitor who had betrayed the *Reichsführer* SS to the Tommies.

The blond officer pushed his way in front of them to where a sobbing, broken Otto lay crumpled on the floor, his face a mess of blood-red gore, holding his broken ribs. 'Stop . . . stop . . .' he commanded, 'there's no more time for that now. The Tommies will be on to us at any minute. Can't you hear . . . They're sounding the escape siren . . . They know something's up . . . Quick, let's dump the treacherous rat in the crapper and get it over with. *Nun macht schom!*'

Suddenly they were all aware of their danger. Eager hands dragged Otto to his feet. He started to scream. To no avail. He was lifted high into the air, as if he weighed no more than a baby. Down below him now was that terrible quaking yellow morass. In a few seconds it would be all over. They would have murdered him in it.

'Get the squeegee,' the blond officer commanded. 'At the double! They'll be here in a minute. We'll push him under and make sure the bastard drowns with that.'

'Squeegee here!' a burly giant cried, holding up the heavy brush with which the latrines were cleaned, his muscles rippling brutally and threatening to burst out of the thin material of his shirt. 'Ready when you are!'

'Now!' the blond officer commanded. 'Ready to let him go!'

'Ready to let him go!' a dozen hoarse voices echoed excitedly.

Otto looked down through the puffed-up slits of rapidly closing eyes.

Below him that yellow mess bubbled and gurgled nauseatingly, the stench almost overpowering. He tried to speak. Nothing came, but meaningless, absurd sounds. His eyes bulged from his poor beaten face as if they might well explode from his eye-sockets at the very next moment.

The blond officer raised his right finger and began to count, *'One!'*

'ONE!' they echoed in a gruff bass, as if this were some counting game, the running feet outside momentarily forgotten.

'Two!'

'TWO!' came the echo.

'Th . . .'

The officer's words ended in a scream of absolute agony, as the brass-tipped pacing-stick came hurtling through the hessian screen, like a bolt thrown down from the heavens by some angry God, and struck deep into his skinny chest. For one awesome moment, the blond officer teetered there, hands grasping the shaft that transfixed his body, eyes wild, wide, and full of utter disbelief at this terrible thing which was happening to him. Next instant he fell backwards into that yellow goo. While the others stared in stupefied horror, he began to sink. His shoulders disappeared. Weakly, he tried to tilt his head up out of the way. To no avail! The dread liquid reached up to his chin. His eyes were still open and he was obviously conscious, they could see that. But he made no attempt now to escape; and they were too dumbstruck by this sudden turn of events to do anything to help him. His mouth went under. A flurry of bubbles erupted on the surface of the ordure. He went under again. For a few seconds his pale hand resurfaced, its fingers jerking convulsively. Then it, too, disappeared – and the surface of the pit was still.

Wordlessly and solemnly, as if they were carrying out some long-established and well-known ceremony, the others began to lower Otto to the floor – in the very same instant that a frantic-eyed Moishe MacTavish came running into the latrine, shouting his head off and flourishing his Colt . . .

It was all over.

SEVEN

Outside it drizzled miserably. The raindrops zig-zagged down the window panes like cold tears. It was cold for early summer, and the three of them huddled together on the rubble-littered floor of the abandoned farmhouse, shivering every time a fresh draught of icy air came from under the door. Routinely, his dark, unshaven face set and glum, Moishe MacTavish passed his flask of precious bourbon to the others and Otto and the Count would take a grateful sip. None of them spoke. Each of the comrades appeared wrapped up in his own cocoon of gloomy thoughts.

Otto, draped in the grey army blanket which the eyeless sergeant-major had given him before they had departed the camp (and which, unknown to him at that time, was the very same one that Sergeant-Major Austin had thrown over Himmler's dead body)[1] ached. He ached all over from the beating he had received at the hands of the enraged POWs in the latrine. But not only his body had suffered, Otto felt sick in his mind, too. His very brain felt numb and sore. It hurt even to think. But think he had to.

He thought of all the things he had done, in this war that was finally over. The risks he had taken, the dangers he had suffered, the miseries he had endured – and for what? He was hungry, broke, a man without a country. Why, he hadn't even had a piece of tail since the Amis had recruited him for their damnfool scheme back at the Depot. Not as much as a 'quickie', or a three-minute hand-job. Life was hell!

[1] Perhaps I should have guessed what Otto had been planning all along, when, a couple of years back, after he had learned about the 'Himmler blanket', as he called it, he suggested having them manufactured *en gros*. 'Christ, Leo,' he had exclaimed excitedly, 'the Yanks'd buy them at a hundred dollars a throw! They're crazy about souvenirs.'

Moishe MacTavish's thoughts were hardly less gloomy. Here he was, a deserter from the US army, masquerading as a bird-colonel, lumbered with two Krauts who, nice guys that they were, were scarcely the kind of company that a Jewish-American should be keeping in the summer of 1945. In short, it seemed to him, at that particular moment in time, that Mrs MacTavish's son was well and truly caught by the short and curlies.

Only the Count, sunk in his thoughts as he was, did not appear to be as totally depressed by the situation in which they found themselves this cold dawn. Watching his big flamboyant companion, whose grey hair was a little too long and who made even the gesture of sitting at this ungodly hour of the morning somehow theatrical, Otto remarked sourly, 'Well out with it. What mad scheme are you hatching *now* in that big turnip of yourn?'

The Count was in no way offended by Otto's surly manner. As he had noticed often enough before, working-class people were invariably surly and short-tempered in the early morning; it had to be something to do with their poor diet. 'I was just thinking, Otto, my boy,' he replied mildly enough.

'*Don't!*' Otto snapped. 'A Yiddish deserter, a Berlin working-lad, broke and far from home, with half a dozen cracked ribs, plus yourself, fucked-up as always! No, Count, it just doesn't bear thinking about.'

'*Amen*, Otto,' Moishe agreed miserably and took another drink of his bourbon. 'Holy cow, what a frigging mess!'

The Count beamed at the tired, desperate faces of his two friends. 'Don't despair,' he exclaimed, with a melodramatic swing of his arm, straight from the breast, as if he were about to declaim Lincoln's Gettysburg Address. 'There is still hope. All is not lost. The tribulations of this world are sent to try us, my friends. There are those who bend and finally break under the tremendous strain. Unfortunately, they are the losers in the game of life. But there are others – like ourselves, I make so bold to maintain – who fight back and triumph . . . who do not succumb, who scale the heights that lead out of this vale of tears which –'

'*Count!*' Otto said firmly. 'Will you shitting well *shut up*! You're rabbiting on like a shitting rabbi in the Jew-School!' Otto's hand flew to his mouth. 'Excuse me, Moishe, got carried away.'

Moishe shrugged carelessly. 'No sweat, Otto. The mess I'm in, no self-respecting rabbi would want to pass the time of day with me. Even my own mother'll probably cross to the other side of the street when she sees me again – *if* she sees me again.'

The Count shook his head gently, as if he were a little shocked at the two of them. 'Why such defeatism, my friends?' he asked. 'Do not throw the blunderbuss into the corn yet . . .'

'The blunderbuss into the corn?' Moishe stuttered, bewildered.

'A German expression,' Otto explained hastily. 'It means, don't give up. But what in three devils' name are you getting at, you silly old fart?'

Outside, the miserable drizzle had stopped. As if on cue, with the Almighty himself playing stage director, a burst of sunlight came shining through the window to encircle the Count's silver head, so that it sparkled dazzlingly and made him look as if he were wearing a halo.

'This, Otto. Human beings are not helpless. They are sometimes deflected, deceived, dispirited. So, as long as human beings can persuade themselves they are not creatures of failure, they can look at the world –'

'*COUNT!*' both Moishe and Otto shrieked as one.

At last the older man stopped preaching. He let his shoulders droop, as if he were resigned to the fact that he would always be misunderstood in this 'vale of tears', as he would undoubtedly have called it, and said simply: 'Gertrud'.

Moishe looked at Otto and tapped his temple significantly. 'Poor old bastard,' he whispered, 'it's been a bit too much for him. He's flipped his wig!'

Otto wasn't listening. He snarled, 'What the shit do you mean – *Gertrud*?'

The Count beamed at him. 'She's the answer,' he replied maddeningly.

'*The answer to what?*'

'To our problem. Gertrud is the way you're finally going to achieve that green twig you are always talking about, Otto.'

At last Otto got it. He slapped his head with both hands like a man who was about to go mad – or invent the steam engine. 'Of course . . . of course, why the devil didn't I think of it before. Gertrud! My God, Count, you're a genius. I could shitting well kiss you, you old fart!'

The Count looked modestly at his nails. 'We live in a time of philosophical poverty, my boy,' he said obscurely, while Moishe stared back and forth, first to the Count, looking as smug as a cat which had just swallowed the cream, and then to Otto, whose handsome young face was suddenly bursting with renewed energy, eyes blazing, as his mind raced furiously.

'I . . . I don't get it, guys,' he stuttered in bewilderment. 'What is this . . . Who is this Gertrud broad?'

'*Himmler's mistress!*' Otto exclaimed in delight. 'If anyone should know –'

'Where the loot is,' Moishe beat him to it.

'*IT'LL BE GERTRUD . . .!*' the three of them exclaimed, rolling about suddenly, slapping each other on the back, their misery forgotten, indeed the whole damned war-torn world of summer 1945 forgotten, tears of joy streaming down their flushed, excited faces, as they considered that delightful prospect! *G E R T R U D . . .*

AUTHOR'S NOTE

It is thus that I always like to recollect Otto Stahl these days – after the sensation of the 'Himmler Love Letters', and his subsequent disappearance. In that remote, shell-shattered Schleswig-Holstein farmhouse, smelling of pigs and stale white cabbage. Young and happy and confident, full of that Berlin working-class spirit, sure again that things would work out well; that nothing could go wrong for 'Frau Stahl's handsome son', as he would undoubtedly have phrased it. The Otto Stahl of those last few months in Spain when, as I know now, he was planning his last great coup, venial, cynical and not a little desperate, was not a very pleasant person. And, I must admit, it hurt a lot that he had taken me, his biographer of these last few years, for a ride. Perhaps that, too, is a reason why I prefer the Otto of 1945, still desperately trying to find that 'green twig' which he so fervently sought, to that 'fat cat' of 1985, soaking up the sun in some tax-haven or other, enjoying his millions at last.

Tolstoy once wrote in his great work *War and Peace*, 'I say this to show the inevitability of falsehood in military description, which serves as material for military histories . . . in these histories I came across such accounts that I did not know whether to laugh or cry, remembering that these books are the chief memorials of that epoch and have had millions of readers.' It is, I think, a very apt quote in this context. Most of you who have read thus far must now be asking yourselves: Well, did Otto Stahl find Himmler's mistress – the fabled 'Gertrud' (if she ever existed, naturally) – and if he did, did she possess those love letters which created such a sensation throughout the Western world last autumn?

Quite frankly I do not know. Some of the details that Otto gave me in Spain of the last weeks of Himmler's life do not accord with the known facts. Himmler was *not* arrested in the Number One Interrogation Centre. *Nor* was Montgomery's Chief-of-Intelligence Colonel Ewart present; the colonel in question was a certain Lt. Colonel Murphy. But Sergeant-Major Austin, the corporation dustman did (and does) exist; and the business with the needle and thread being passed through a dying Himmler's tongue is quite genuine. Such minor inaccuracies can, I feel sure, be put down to the passage of time and the weakness of an old man's memory.

No, the key issue is still, was there a Gertrud and did she possess Himmler's love letters to her? Those of you who followed the BBC's ten-part semi-historical documentary on the subject this spring – *Heinrich and Gertrud: a Nazi Love Affair* will know, of course, that the celebrated English historian and German-specialist, David Irving, vouched personally (in the introduction to the series) that the letter shown to him, dated March 1945, was in the *Reichsführer*'s handwriting. Mr Irving also produced evidence that Himmler had had a previous mistress and in his, Mr Irving's, usual painstaking manner showed the viewers no fewer than eighty receipts from Martin Bormann for Himmler's mortgage contributions[1], in payment for the house he had bought the woman in question.

But Mr Irving's undoubtedly valuable evidence related to *one* letter only. What about the other hundred-odd? Could Heinrich Himmler, such a dried-up individual with so little imagination, really have pleaded with Gertrud to allow him to wear her 'best black lace knickers' the next time he visited her? (Letter No. 82, dated 11 November 1943). Could he have joked, a little further on in the same letter, that he wanted to feel black silk next to his skin because it was '*Heldengedenktag*' when the war[2] dead should be 'honoured in a special way, ha, ha!' Would anyone at the time have attributed such a macabre sense of humour to the *Reichsführer*, if that is what it was?

[1] See D. Irving: *Himmler's Mortgage: the True Story*, Weidenfeld & Nicolson, Illustrated, £25.50. 1984.

[2] The German equivalent of Armistice Day.

What does one make, too, of that most notorious letter, written on 22 June 1941, the day Hitler invaded Russia, which, as everyone knows, caused such a sensation when it first appeared in the *News of the World* under the banner headline:

Secretary Reveals All. Raped On A Fur Rug. Exclusive!

'What madness. A married man, with children. Carried away with such passion, and you not even a Party Member, my beloved Gertrud! But I had to possess you, there and then, even if it were on the experimental fur coat (imitation rabbit) being produced for our brave fellows soon to march into Russia and defeat the red hordes. You had to be mine. What delicious joy when you surrendered and became really mine at last!'

'*For ever*', someone had written in purple ink in the margin of the yellowing, wartime paper. Presumably the fabled Gertrud. What a field day the *News of the World* had that Sunday, with a seven-foot tall model in sheer black stockings – and nothing else – reeling back onto a spread of silver fox, the size of a football pitch, before another model in bulging Y-fronts, wielding a whip! (Male, of course.) There were even questions in the House on how far a newspaper might go in such matters.

But could Himmler really have written such stuff, never mind having indulged in that kind of office high-jinks? Weren't The Letters clever fakes after all, the products of Otto Stahl's undoubtedly vivid imagination, aided perhaps by the former owner of what he himself called the 'Jewish Mills & Boon', Marty MacTavish, presently being sought by the New York police because of the million dollars worth of debts that he left behind when he fled the States so suddenly?

I really don't know. All that I can offer in evidence in Otto's favour that The Letters were not a total fake is this: an indistinct colour snapshot, probably taken by a Polaroid camera. It shows a group of happy, laughing people beneath a grove of waving palm trees, standing on what looks like a white beach. In the centre of the jolly group is a very old man seated in a wheelchair, being watched attentively by a plump, very much younger woman. There is no mistaking the old man. Even in his dotage, there is that ham actor's pose about him, which Otto hated so much during the war. To left and right of the armchair there stands a grinning sunburned Marty MacTavish, one arm around the waist of the nubile, half-naked native girl, who could well be his grand-daughter. Otto is on the other side, his eyes full of that triumphant German *schadenfreude*, a malicious smile on his lips, as he holds up a green palm frond. It is that 'green twig', naturally, to which he aspired all his long and slightly crooked life. Otto wanted me to get the message.

But it is the dedication and the signatures which go with it that are the really important things about the snap. The dedication is in Otto's habitual, crude style. *'The Devil, they say in Kraut, always shits on the biggest heap, Leo. We've pulled it off at last – and I don't mean what your dirty mind might be thinking, Leo. Love, Otto, Marty, the Count'* – and then in purple ink in that flowing hand, familiar to those who have read the comments penned by Himmler's fabled mistress on the margins of The Letters – *'Gertrud von der Weide'*.

'Gertrud von der Weide!' When I first saw that signature, it struck me with the impact of a bomb. Had they really found her back in 1945? And had the Count finally married her? Somehow I never thought Graf von der Weide was the marrying kind. Still, there it is – er – purple on white, so to speak. *'Gertrud von der Weide.'*

Is it the same Gertrud? Had she kept Himmler's love letters after all? Why is it that such sensational material was hidden for over forty years? What role did Otto, the petty crook, and Marty, the failed publisher, play in the whole strange affair? Where had the Count been all these years? Why did Otto, during the three or four years of our working association, always lead me to believe that the 'silly old fart', as he invariably called Graf von der Weide, was long dead?

So many questions with so few answers. Yet, one thing,

I think, is sure, gentle reader. This. We have not yet heard the end of 'Frau Stahl's handsome son'. One day, I am absolutely certain of this, Otto Stahl will become bored with that remote desert island, even if it is populated with nubile dusky beauties, who have apparently not yet heard of the bra. He will return to his old hunting grounds here in Europe. Let us hope that day is not too far away. Otto, come back! Please. As you would phrase it, '*We shitting well miss you*'.

Leo Kessler, Wittlich, Germany, November 1984.

OTTO'S PHONEY WAR

Otto Stahl 1

Leo Kessler

ON THE NIGHT HITLER'S PANZERS ROARED INTO POLAND, OTTO WAS WORKING UNDERCOVER WITH THE SERGEANT'S WIFE.

Crook, conman, casanova, blue-eyed Otto Stahl is equally at home with an eager fraulein or a batch of black market coffee. A natural coward with a genius for saving his own skin, Otto dodges the German draft – only to be catapulted into frontline action against the Dutch tank regiments.

Decorated by Hitler, stripped by Himmler, seduced by a nymphomaniac Countess, and relentlessly pursued by SS headhunters, Otto bluffs his way from bedroom to battlefield and back.

The bawdy, bloody and hilarious adventures of one man's war which tells the inside story of the Third Reich as it has never been told before!

FUTURA PUBLICATIONS
FICTION/WAR
0 7088 2027 1

OTTO'S BLITZKRIEG!

Otto Stahl 2

Leo Kessler

CONTINUING THE BAWDY, BLOODY AND HILARIOUS ADVENTURES OF THE GREATEST CONMAN AND CASANOVA IN THE GERMAN ARMY: OTTO'S BLITZKRIEG!

ONLY OTTO STAHL COULD TURN CAPTURE IN A MOBILE BROTHEL INTO BECOMING A HERO OF THE THIRD REICH.

Safely tucked away in a mobile field brothel in the north of France, Otto thought he had the rest of the war sewn up. Until the night commandoes raided the coast and whisked Otto off to a POW camp in England. But, resourceful as ever, Otto cons his way out and home to Germany – to a hero's unwelcome honour of a special assignment from the Führer himself.

FUTURA PUBLICATIONS
FICTION/WAR
0 7088 2173 1

OTTO AND THE SS

Otto Stahl 5

Leo Kessler

HERR OTTO STAHL HAS DONE IT AGAIN! IN *OTTO AND THE SS* HE REVEALS YET ANOTHER SENSATIONAL CHAPTER OF HIS EXTRAORDINARY WAR MEMOIRS.

It is Berlin in 1944 and, courtesy of the black market, Otto and his mate, The Count, are having an easy time . . . until the military police strike! Saved from detection by an ageing whore, they prudently decide to rejoin the Fatherland in its fight for glory.

So, as volunteers in Hitler's extraordinary Ardennes offensive, they masquerade in US uniforms and, under the code names Mex and Tex, proceed to spread mayhem amongst the enemy . . . in a last ditch attempt to seize the bridges over the Meuse.

Bloody, bawdy and always funny, Otto Stahl's memoirs offer a never-before-seen inside look at Hitler's Great War.

FUTURA PUBLICATIONS
FICTION/WAR
0 7088 2376 9